"You are so beautiful, little Victorine, that any man would kneel at your feet. I shall need all of my skill as a swordsman to fight off your other suitors."

Victorine's head swam. She felt a quivering in her stomach, and her heart beat very fast. She had dreamed of this for years, her first romance, her first love, but the reality was more exciting than she had ever imagined. And yet, she had been flirted with before. How much did André's compliments mean?

"Your words are sweet, Monsieur Valmont," she said softly. "Is your heart as true as your words are polished?"

André's dark eyes flashed; Victorine held her breath. "You doubt the worth of my affections? *Mais non*, Mademoiselle, you shall see what it is to be courted by André Valmont."

As if his statement alone were not enough to make her breath come fast, he leaned forward. Victorine's eyes widened.

He lifted her hand again and this time turned it to kiss her gloved palm. Even through her thin glove, the warm pressure of his lips made her tremble. His dark lashes were long and thick, and his lips were smooth —how would it be to kiss such a man? It was a daring thought. Victorine shivered again.

Don't miss any of the books in
SOUTHERN ANGELS—
a four-title historical romance series from
Bantam Books!

Elizabeth Stafford, Victorine LaGrande, the
slave Hannah, Rosamund Brigham—all
young women from the South, all caught in
the turmoil of the Civil War, all fighting for
their beliefs and for the men
they love.

Southern Angels

WINDS

of

BETRAYAL

CHERYL ZACH

BANTAM BOOKS

New York Toronto London Sydney Auckland

*For Stephanie, Wishes you an special "good friend" angel...
babuy Hawaiian Amiges. Love always— Chryl Zach '95*

RL 6.6, age 012 and up

WINDS OF BETRAYAL
A Bantam Book / August 1995

ISBN 0-553-56218-5

Published simultaneously in the United States and Canada

PRINTED IN THE UNITED STATES OF AMERICA

OPM   0 9 8 7 6 5 4 3 2 1

This book is dedicated, with love, to my aunts Peggy LeGate, Ruth Foster, and Ivagene Le-Gate, and to the memory of my uncles Owen LeGate and Weston LeGate, and to their children and grandchildren.

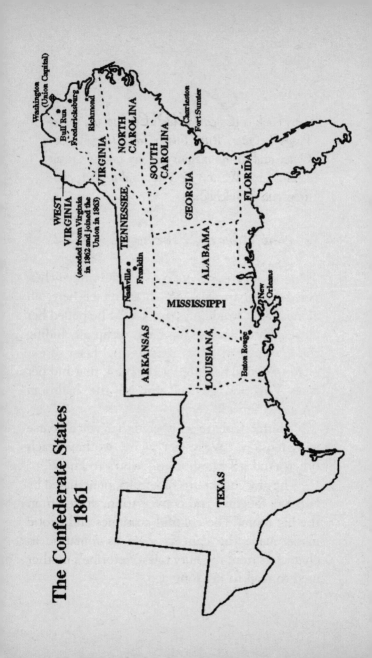

The Confederate States 1861

Washington (Union Capital)
Bull Run
Fredericksburg
Richmond

WEST VIRGINIA
(seceded from Virginia in 1862 and joined the Union in 1863)

VIRGINIA

NORTH CAROLINA

SOUTH CAROLINA

Charleston
Fort Sumter

TENNESSEE

GEORGIA

FLORIDA

Nashville
Franklin

ALABAMA

MISSISSIPPI

New Orleans

ARKANSAS

LOUISIANA

Baton Rouge

TEXAS

Chapter 1

"This is madness," Victorine LaGrande whispered to her friend. "We shouldn't be here, all alone. What would my papa say?" She pulled her cloak tighter against the cool, damp air, hiding the low-cut ball dress that she had been so excited to don. Thankful for the mask that hid her face, Victorine glanced toward the ballroom through the wide veranda doors.

"Hush," Colette whispered, her voice hoarse with tension. "We're not alone; we have each other. And it's Mardi Gras—who's to know?"

The graceful strains of a waltz, punctuated by bursts of laughter and conversation, drifted from the big room. The colorful costumes and exotic masks made the dancers seem as romantic as characters from the fairy tales Victorine's mother used to read to her long ago.

1

But something felt wrong—and not just the fact that they had no invitation to this ball. None of the well-dressed matrons in the ballroom were familiar to her, nor any of the stunningly beautiful young women, many dark-haired and dark-eyed. And Colette had been so mysterious about the whole affair, urging her to come but refusing to give her any details.

Victorine had hesitated when Colette Dubois, her oldest friend, had pleaded with her. Then Victorine had thought of her American friends from Madame Corday's Academy for Young Ladies in Charleston. Elizabeth and Rosamund didn't think it strange to go out without the chaperone always required of respectable Creole girls. Daring Elizabeth would consider this secret ball a lark, Victorine knew. And Rosamund had spirit, too. After all, hadn't those two crouched on a Charleston rooftop while windowpanes rattled and Southern cannons shelled Fort Sumter? They both had courage, as did Hannah, the quiet slave girl who had accompanied Elizabeth to Charleston and been her friend since childhood. Victorine, on the other hand, had been too frightened to watch. Now the memory made her feel ashamed.

Victorine was tired of being the laggard, the one left behind. So tonight, Victorine had come along with Colette, excited over this forbidden adventure.

Victorine looked again through the veranda doors at the throng on the dance floor. The men seemed eager to bow over the hands of the ladies. One young man in particular—lithe of figure, his evening clothes very fine—caught her eye.

His dark hair had been combed smoothly, but a rebellious curl at his temple made Victorine want to smooth it lovingly, and his smile made her stomach quiver. He was the handsomest man she had ever seen. If she could be on the dance floor smiling up at him, instead of skulking outside, then this secret excursion would be worth the risk.

But he already had a beautiful lady on his arm, and he seemed intent on his partner's sparkling dark eyes and the laughing curve of her mouth.

If she hadn't been so impatient, Victorine told herself, her first Mardi Gras ball would have been much more decorous. She could have come into the party on her papa's arm, as a seventeen-year-old young lady should. Her first excitement faded now into renewed apprehension. How had she allowed Colette to talk her into such a wild scrape?

She had always dreamed of her first Mardi

Gras. Before she had left her home to attend Madame Corday's Academy, Victorine had been too young to attend the balls. But she remembered her parents dressing to attend grand Creole parties before her mother and sister had died of yellow fever and her father, fearful for the health of his last child, had sent her away.

But now that civil war had come, Charleston did not seem so safe. The decades-old simmering quarrel about states' rights and slavery, the conflict between the increasingly industrialized North and the agricultural South, had boiled over with the election of Abraham Lincoln. South Carolina had seceded first, followed by other Southern states, and the Confederacy was born. After the fall of Fort Sumter in the spring of 1861 had been followed by the great fire that destroyed much of Charleston in December, Victorine's father had summoned her home to New Orleans.

"There he is!" Colette hissed, clutching Victorine's arm.

Victorine winced. "*Comment?* Who?"

"My brother-in-law!"

Victorine peered at the stocky young man whom Colette pointed out. "But that's not your sister."

"Mais non," Colette agreed, her tone grim. "It's not."

Her eyes widening, Victorine digested the implications. "Are you sure it's Pierre? He's wearing a mask."

"I know him. One shoulder droops a little, you see? And that awful red waistcoat—it's Pierre, *je t'assure*." Watching the dancer in question bow deeply over his partner's hand, Victorine could understand her friend's distress. "That was why you wanted to come tonight? Does your sister know?"

"She suspects—he spends so much time away from home. Every time I go to see her, she's in tears. And they've been married only a year!"

Colette sobbed, then swallowed audibly. "My *maman* says that all the young men do it, until honor demands they put aside these women when they marry. But some do not."

Victorine shook her head in sympathy. But her unease had increased. "Colette, we must go, *tout de suite*."

Colette sighed. *"Oui, je regrette.* I should not have begged you to come, but I had to see for myself."

As Victorine turned, she gasped in alarm. A large, bearded man, his face flushed from too much wine, blocked her way. He wore a purple cloak over his evening suit, and a discarded devil's mask hung on strings below his double chin.

"You're not leaving already? The party's just beginning." He reached for her hand. Victorine drew back in alarm, but he captured her hand in its kid glove. She tried to pull away, but his grip tightened, hurting her fingers.

"Such a trim figure, and such lustrous hair. Won't you lift that mask so that I can see your face?"

"Mais non," Victorine cried sharply. "Let go of me!"

"Now, now, no need for such airs. Is this not why you're here—hoping to find a protector? Where's your *maman*—your chaperone?"

Victorine looked helplessly at Colette.

The stout man leered at them unpleasantly. "What? Here alone, little birds? Is this bait? I'm willing to trip the snare." He pulled Victorine toward him.

She smelled the heavy odor of alcohol, saw the red veins in his eyes as he bent down. Beneath his whiskers, his lips were thick and moist. Fear gave her new strength; she jerked back, pulling her hand from the glove and leaving it empty in his grasp.

"Run!" she called to her friend. "Run for

your life, *mon amie*." Picking up her full skirts, Victorine ran pell-mell for the street.

Behind her she heard the heavy tread of her unwanted suitor.

They were only a stone's throw from the great cathedral, but it stood dark and empty at this time of night. Their homes were a few blocks away in the Vieux Carré, the older French section of the city. As she ran, Victorine's whalebone stays cut deeply into her sides, and her breath came ragged and short. This was no costume for running, even had she been in the practice. Then she stepped on a loose stone in the street and cried out in pain.

"What is it?" Colette grabbed her arm, or Victorine would have fallen. Her ankle had turned, and the pain now cut through her whole body.

"My ankle. Oh, we're lost. Save yourself, Colette. I knew I shouldn't have come." Victorine gasped at the pain in her ankle, all the while peering over her shoulder. The man in the gaudy purple cape was still behind them, puffing a little, his pace slow but stubborn.

"Hurry," Colette urged. "He's coming closer."

A distant scream of laughter echoed down the dark narrow street, along with the faint hum

7

of music. Victorine tried to run, but managed only a few more steps. The sharp pinch of her corset stays cut into her side again, and her ankle throbbed. She clutched her silk face mask grimly, choking back a sob. So this was Mardi Gras!

Seeking concealment, she pushed against a wrought-iron gate that led to a walled courtyard, but it was locked securely. She and Colette crouched under the shadow of an overhanging balcony. Victorine could smell the sour stench of garbage, mixed with old cooking odors and the distant smell of the river. She covered her nose with her perfumed handkerchief.

"He sees us," Colette hissed. "*Mon Dieu!* I will get help."

Victorine bit back a protest as Colette lifted her hoop skirts and darted out into the street. Victorine felt very alone. Then she heard the uneven footsteps come closer.

The man stood before her, staring into the dark shadow where Victorine trembled, frozen with fear.

"There you are, my pretty. Why run away? I just wanted a k-kiss. It's Mardi Gras." The beefy man grinned broadly. He had lost his mask, and his eyes were red and unfocused.

Victorine thought of screaming, but she was too frightened to draw a deep breath. If this got out, her reputation would be ruined. And her father's anger and shock—it was too awful to think on. But she'd rather die right here than kiss the fleshy face of this leering stranger. He gripped her cloak and pulled her closer, ripping away her mask with a rough hand.

Panic-stricken, Victorine pushed him with all her strength. While he reeled backward, she slipped out of his grasp and ran. But after only a few steps, her ankle twisted again, and she fell to the ground. The impact took her breath. The paving stones were cold and gritty against her cheek, and she felt a sharp twinge of pain in her shoulder.

The man stumbled after her, leaning over her tangled skirts. She smelled his liquor-tainted breath.

Victorine screamed.

Then the man was abruptly pulled backward. She heard the solid thud of a blow. The big man collapsed at her feet.

Astonished, she stared at the prone body. She could see the whites of his eyes and his slack mouth. Standing above him was a tall man who had knocked down her attacker. She drew a deep breath, struggling between relief and fear.

"Are you hurt?" Her rescuer held out his

hand and helped her up. His accent was American. "There's blood on your cheek."

Victorine touched her face and gasped when she saw the scarlet stain on her fingers. Tears slipped from her eyes, and she struggled for control. Her ankle hurt fiercely, and she was sore all over from her fall.

"It's my ankle especially," she whispered.

"Let me see."

Victorine drew a deep breath. Show a man her ankle? What was he thinking of? Was this man as dissolute as the drunk who had pursued them from the party?

"I'm a doctor," the man told her gravely. "It's all right."

Uncertain, Victorine bit her lip. The stranger knelt before her and waited. Timidly she lifted her long skirts slightly and put out her small foot.

He examined the foot and ankle, probing gently, and Victorine gasped. But even in her pain, she could feel how warm his fingers were through her silk stockings, and how gentle his touch. She had never had a man touch her like this.

She risked a quick glance down at his bent head. His hat covered most of his dark blond hair. His composure made him seem very mature, but his voice did not sound old, and there was strength to spare in the way he had so neatly disposed of the drunk.

"No bones broken. Time will tell how bad the sprain is," he told her, rising. "I'll see you safely home; then you must soak the limb and wrap it tightly."

Victorine looked away, new worries crowding her mind. If this stranger took her home, he could find out her name. A scandal would ruin her forever. And what about her father?

Yet Colette still hadn't returned, and Victorine was in no shape to be left alone again, with drunken revelers roaming the streets. She accepted the doctor's arm and leaned against him as she hobbled along.

"Do your parents know that you're out this late, alone?" he asked quietly. "I know it's carnival time, but you are too young to be unescorted."

Victorine bit her lip. How could she explain?

"Victorine!" someone shrieked. Colette hurried toward her, another figure behind her. "You are safe?"

Victorine nodded, wishing her friend would hold her tongue. "*Mais oui*, it's only my ankle. This gentleman was kind enough to assist me. He has offered to escort me home." She hoped Colette would catch the unease in her tone; he must not be allowed to see where they lived.

Colette stared at the stranger, her curiosity evident. "I can help you now. And Henri will see us home."

The man with Colette was the Dubois family's black butler, Henri. He had hastily pulled on his trousers over his nightshirt. His coat was unbuttoned, and his bare feet seemed lost in the overlarge shoes—probably hand-me-downs from his master. He nodded, his dark face solemn.

"Got to make tracks, you hear? You young'uns should be home in bed."

Victorine withdrew her hand from the security of the doctor's arm. She gazed at him anxiously. Would he insist on accompanying them?

But he seemed to guess the direction of her thoughts. His lips curved. "Remember what I said about soaking your ankle," he reminded her, "and I hope you'll choose your friends more carefully next time."

As if that fat leech were a friend! Victorine flushed in annoyance. "I shall," she said pointedly. Then she felt ashamed of her lack of gratitude. He had come to her aid, after all, and behaved with true courtesy. "Thank you for your kindness, sir," she said formally, holding out her hand.

His grip was light but firm as he shook her hand, then tipped his hat and said good-night. As she watched the young doctor walk away, she felt a curious regret. Would she ever see him again?

Nonsense, Victorine chided herself a moment later. *He's a stranger and an American—nothing to me.*

"Let's go," she told Colette, leaning on her friend's shoulder and limping as quickly as she could toward home.

For hundreds of years, New Orleans's Creole families had lived and worked in stately seclusion, cherishing their European roots, ignoring the too-bold, too-loud American settlers pushing their way into the old city. Creoles lived apart, in their own society. This was the way it had been, and this was the way it would always be.

Or could the war that raged across the South disrupt this ordered and restricted way of life? Some Creoles seemed to think this was possible, though Victorine herself refused to believe it. Suddenly she felt a moment of dizziness, as if the ground had slipped a little beneath her. She was being silly, upset by her close escape.

She turned to her friend. "I'll never listen to you again," she whispered to Colette. "What a nightmare!"

"C'est la vie." Her friend gave a shrug. "But it turned out all right. Henri won't tell on us, and no one heard me slip into the back of the courtyard to fetch him from the slave quarters."

Victorine shook her head. Her fear had turned to anger. "It was folly, Colette!"

"You've lost your mask," Colette whispered. Her face was still hidden behind hers. Victorine had forgotten all about her mask. Would the doctor recognize her face if he saw her again? It was unlikely; New Orleans was a big city. Besides, Creoles, descendants of old French families, rarely met the newer American residents in New Orleans socially. She bit her lip in worry nonetheless.

"Oh well, the mayor would be happy." Colette giggled.

"Pourquoi?"

"Remember, he ordered no parades this year and no masking in the street. He's afraid the Union army will sneak into the city masked as Mardi Gras revelers." Colette laughed quietly.

But Victorine had witnessed Union forces at war while she was at school in Charleston. The sight of cannon smoke darkening the sky haunted her still. *"Mon Dieu!* I pray it will not be so."

"Silly, the Yankees will never take New Orleans," Colette argued. "Our city is such an important port, sitting near the mouth of the Mississippi—the Confederacy would never allow it to be captured. That's why General Lovell is here, why so many men are drilling, *oui?* With the earthworks and the ditches, and the forts to guard the river, we are safe. Besides, our European allies would protest any invasion, too; your father has said so."

Victorine gazed at the houses that lined the dark street, its quiet broken by occasional echoes of music, laughter, and shouts that marked another Mardi Gras party. Abruptly she shivered.

"I hope you're right," she whispered.

Chapter 2

"Are you ready, *ma petite?*"

"Papa!" Victorine hurried to open her bedroom door. "Do you like my new gown?"

"Elle est belle, n'est-ce pas?" Tante Marie waved her fan in excitement. A spinster, Victorine's aunt had come gladly for an extended visit from her brother's home on a Louisiana plantation. Tante Marie had the same gentle voice and kind heart as her dead sister, Victorine's *maman.* Victorine smiled at her aunt, then turned back to her father.

She whirled, enjoying the swish of silken petticoats and the heavier rustle of her brocade skirt. Her ball gown was a glorious sight indeed. The scarlet brocade bodice was low-cut, trimmed with gold embroidery. Her matching scarlet pelisse was lined with white ermine, with wide bands at the bottom.

Victorine's maidservant, Soozie, stood back, a hairbrush in her hand, beaming with pride as her mistress displayed the result of their hours of preparation.

"You look like a princess." Monsieur LaGrande kissed her forehead lightly. "I missed you, *ma petite*, while you were away at school. This old house was very quiet. Look, I brought you something to wear tonight, at your first Mardi Gras ball."

For a moment, Victorine looked away. She'd tried to push back the memory of her ridiculous escapade of a week ago; only her ankle's lingering soreness reminded her. Papa must never discover what had happened.

Now she focused on the black velvet box her father held out. When he flipped open the lid, she had no trouble forgetting her worries. She gasped. "Oh, Papa! *Très jolies!*" She touched the ruby and diamond eardrops with one reverent finger.

"They were your *maman*'s. I thought they would look very fine with your gown." Her father spoke softly.

Her aunt cooed over the jewelry, but Victorine's vision blurred as she remembered her gentle, beautiful mother, who had died too young of yellow fever. She blinked away the tears, determined not to be sad tonight. "I will treasure them doubly."

She went back to her looking glass to position the earrings carefully, then slipped into her pelisse and paused while her maid adjusted one strand of Victorine's dark hair.

"Such a shame Colette took a chill and can't go tonight," her aunt murmured.

Victorine swallowed hard. "A pity," she agreed, accepting her father's arm. Tante Marie followed behind.

"I will escort the most beautiful lady at the ball," her father boasted, smiling. "The young men will be jealous, n'est-ce pas? There is one young man in particular whom I want you to meet."

Blushing, Victorine knew her smile was wide. All her life she had waited for this moment, her first Mardi Gras ball. That prank a week ago didn't count, she told herself fiercely. Tonight she would walk in on her papa's arm and meet the handsome prince she had always dreamed of. Her happiness was just beginning. The ball would be delightful, her life would be a series of pleasant events—surely the sadness was all behind her.

Victorine squeezed her father's arm. Balancing her heavy skirts, she walked slowly down the stairway.

When they entered the ballroom inside the

house across town, Victorine paused while her father handed his top hat to the dark-skinned footman. She had already shed her pelisse, peeking into a looking glass to check her elaborate coiffure.

The folding doors had been thrown back to combine the family's two parlors into one large salon for the party. Victorine glanced at the marble fireplace and the rosewood furniture upholstered in expensive crimson silk. Crystal chandeliers hung from the ceiling, and the walls held oil paintings of generations of ancestors, tracing their host's Creole lineage back to the usual minor French aristocracy.

Victorine's heart beat rapidly; she could hear the rollicking music and the chatter of partygoers thronging the wide salon. She was glad that Creole ladies did not normally wear masks; she was too eager to see the ensemble to wish to peer through narrow eyeholes. Tonight she wanted to see it all!

"You remember Mademoiselle Marie de Castillon, my late wife's sister, and my daughter, Victorine LaGrande." Her father had paused to speak to a couple near the door, both gray-haired and very elegant in their dress.

She had not heard the rest of the introduction, but Victorine curtsied to the couple.

"Ah, so nice to see you again, *ma chérie*," the woman said. "How you have grown! You look so much like your dear mother."

"*Merci, madame*," Victorine murmured.

"You must allow our son to have the pleasure of a dance; where is that rascal?" She looked around the big ballroom.

But another couple was waiting behind them. Monsieur LaGrande shook his head. "Bring him over when you find him, Louisa. We are holding up the late arrivals."

He led Victorine and Tante Marie farther into the room and found narrow gilt chairs for them. Tante Marie settled herself comfortably and turned to gossip with the older lady sitting beside her.

But Victorine didn't want to sit down. The music was gay, and she found her foot tapping eagerly. The movement caused a twinge in her injured ankle; despite herself she remembered the American doctor's fingers probing it gently. His touch had been so warm and so strong. But that was another forbidden memory. Already there were couples moving smoothly on the dance floor. Would no one ask her to dance?

Her father smiled, as if reading her thoughts. "Would you allow your papa to have the first dance?"

"Oh yes." Victorine flashed her father a wide smile, then followed him decorously onto the floor. As a child, she had watched her parents sway gracefully together. Her father was only a little taller than Victorine, and she could see the streaks of gray at his temples. They moved smoothly through the set while the gaslights flickered against the gilt-papered walls and the perfumes of the dancers blended into a heady mixture of scent. She could feel the new eardrops gently brushing her neck as she glided across the hardwood floor. *What a magical evening,* Victorine thought.

When the tune ended, her father bowed to her and led her back to the edge of the dance floor.

"Rudolf," someone called to Monsieur LaGrande. An older man with a V-shaped beard approached.

"Excuse me for a moment, *ma petite,*" her father said.

Unwillingly Victorine sat down on one of the narrow chairs, full skirts cascading around her. She was too impatient to sit still. Beneath her concealing gown, her feet mimicked the dance steps as the musicians struck up a new tune. She didn't want to waste a moment of this party.

"You look like a goddess of the night," a masculine voice said. "A wood nymph who has wandered into the city by chance. Can such beauty belong to a mortal girl?"

Startled, Victorine turned to find a slim young man of medium height standing beside her. His face looked familiar, and his smile was both lofty and intriguing.

"You are too kind," she said formally, remembering what her *maman* had taught her. "But we have not been introduced." His dark eyes flashed, and the roguish smile curved even deeper.

"Do I need an introduction to a goddess? Shall I not bow in humble subjection to your beauty instead? Or throw myself into the sea in sacrifice if you choose not to smile upon me?"

"Silly," Victorine murmured, but she flushed at the outrageous compliments. Then a memory reappeared, and she held her breath. This was the striking young man she had glimpsed at the secret ball, the one with the beautiful girl on his arm. She looked away, gripping her fan so tightly that she heard a delicate ivory rib crack.

"Have I offended you?" the young man asked. "If so, I beg your pardon. But beauty can, indeed, overcome caution."

"No, no," Victorine muttered, shaking her

head but still not daring to look into his dark eyes.

"You see, I kneel before you, overcome with contrition."

She couldn't help raising her gaze. It was true; he knelt on the wood floor, to the detriment of his expensive trousers.

She blushed again; people were already staring. "*Mais non*, do get up," she begged. "The gossip—we will be laughed at. Get up at once, *s'il vous plaît*."

He rose, but she saw him grimace. "*Non, non*, my wood nymph. No one would dare to laugh. The ruffian would receive my challenge before he had closed his mouth; we would meet at dawn, and he would never laugh again!"

A duel? Victorine opened her eyes wide. Throughout her childhood, she had heard endless gossip of hot-blooded encounters in the Crescent City, of secret fights with pistols or swords to avenge a real or imagined offense.

He took her hand, pressed it between his own. "Do not look so alarmed, little nymph. No one would dare to offend me; my reputation with the sword and the pistol is too great."

She could feel the warmth of his hand through the thin gloves, and her own heart beating faster. Was this the handsome prince she had always dreamed of—this dashing young stranger with his outrageous remarks? Had she walked into her fantasy?

In her daydreams, she would have flirted back, said exactly the right thing to captivate a worldly young man. But the memory of the forbidden ball slowed her thoughts, and her usual ready answer had disappeared. She looked down at her small hand still gripped firmly in both of his, and was silent.

"Still worried about the lack of formal introduction, *ma belle*? Shall I remedy this small omission?" His tone was laughing again; she felt young and foolish.

"*Voilà!* André, you have already met the lovely Victorine!" The elegant gray-haired lady who had earlier greeted Victorine and her father sailed up, her lavender dress with its full skirts as majestic as a clipper ship gliding over a smooth sea.

"Indeed, I could not miss the most beautiful lady at our ball," André agreed, his tone almost too formal.

Victorine wondered if he was laughing at her just a little, but all doubt disappeared as the introduction was performed. "My son, the redoubtable André Valmont," his mother said, her tone wry. "Make your bow to Mademoiselle LaGrande."

Valmont? *This* was the young man about whom her papa had hinted? Victorine blinked, then tried not to smile. She could tell Madame Valmont that her son had already been on his knees to her, but she blushed at even considering such a bold statement, true though it was. How foolish she had been, objecting to the attentions of the most eligible bachelor at the party. The Valmonts were old friends of her parents, and their wealth and social prestige in the Creole community rivaled her own family's.

Her father hurried to join them. "I see you have found your missing heir," Monsieur LaGrande said, smiling. "Have you met my daughter, then, André?"

"It is my great pleasure," André agreed. "But I should be even happier if she would allow me the honor of a dance."

"*Bien sûr,*" Monsieur LaGrande agreed before Victorine had time to answer. To his daughter, he said, "You will find André a most accomplished dancer, *ma petite.*"

Her cheeks still hot, Victorine nodded and allowed André to escort her onto the dance floor.

"Happy now, *ma belle?*" André bowed over her hand.

Victorine smiled briefly and did not answer as they glided through the intricate pattern of the dance. André was, indeed, a polished dancer, and she must not look clumsy in comparison. Not until the music died did she look up into his dark eyes again. She detected a gleam of mischief there.

"You are as graceful as you are beautiful, my wood nymph. Would you care to stroll in the courtyard?"

"Perhaps. But do you expect me to turn into a tree?" Victorine fluttered her dark lashes, flipping open her fan. She would not allow him to see that the thought of being alone in the darkness with this young gallant made her stomach tighten. Despite her papa's approval, despite her own racing pulse, she would not make André Valmont's courtship too simple a task.

André laughed. "Your beauty seems more than mortal, mademoiselle. I would not be surprised to see you sprout leaves."

"To avoid your pursuit?" Victorine raised her fan to hide her smile. "I trust you will give me no reason to do so?"

"No, indeed," André said quickly. "You are safe with me, always." Then his dark eyes sparkled as he detected the smile she didn't quite hide. "You rogue, you make sport of me! Come, we shall walk in the courtyard."

Picking up her skirts with one hand, she laid the other in the curve of his arm. As they walked through the open veranda doors, she saw several couples enjoying the moonlight and a matron or two acting as chaperones.

Lush potted plants framed the brick courtyard, and the air was heavy with moisture. The faint breath of a breeze cooled Victorine's cheeks and bare shoulders. Green vines encircled the white pillars of the piazza and made lacy patterns on the walls of the house, while green window shutters stood open to catch the air. The large leaves of a banana tree fluttered, and a fountain splashed merrily in the center. Flower beds edged the wall. André nodded toward a bench. "Shall we sit?"

Victorine had been enjoying the cool air, but now she lifted her brows. "I should not linger too long without my aunt or papa," she demurred. This was not Charleston, she must remember; Creole girls were strictly chaperoned at all times.

"I think your papa would be pleased at anything we did," André argued, a gleam in his dark eyes. "But I will not distress you; you are young yet, and innocent, as you should be."

Victorine frowned. She was seventeen, after

27

all, a young lady. "I am not distressed," she declared flatly. Holding her head high, she walked across the brick courtyard and sank gracefully to the bench.

Victorine saw a couple leaning close together, the young man whispering to his sweetheart. "André," she murmured, "that gentleman is in uniform. Are many here signing up for service to the Confederacy?"

André shrugged. "*Mais oui*, it's all the rage, these volunteer companies. But a waste of time. The Yankees will never take New Orleans."

"He looks very fine," Victorine murmured, using her fan skillfully.

André had lost his smile. "His trousers do not hang well," he pointed out, "and his jacket is too tight."

Victorine refused to be distracted by the fit of the young man's uniform. "But so brave! One must admire their courage. I saw Fort Sumter bombarded from the windows of my school, did you know, when the great war began."

"No place for a lady to be," André objected. "Were you not frightened?"

"Oh yes. We could feel the schoolhouse shaking." Victorine shivered, remembering. "My friends climbed out on the roof to watch, but I could not bear to stay."

28

"*Mon Dieu*, I should think not." André nodded approval. "Who expects a lady to show courage? That is for men."

To her surprise, Victorine felt a flicker of annoyance. *Don't I have the right to support my homeland?* she thought. *Still, a lady does not argue with a gentleman.*

"Southern ladies are to be protected, adored," André was explaining. "My wife—she will be the most pampered of creatures, as it should be, *non?*"

The thought—the merest suggestion—of being the wife of the handsome and dashing André Valmont was enough to make Victorine forget everything else. She felt her cheeks go hot, and she stared down at the bricks beneath her feet.

André's voice was gentle now. He reached to take her hand. "Have I frightened you, *ma petite?* Do not be alarmed. Would it be such a dreadful fate, to be Madame André Valmont?"

"*Non, non,*" Victorine murmured, very conscious of the gentle pressure of his touch. She could not meet his gaze. He was so handsome that her thoughts scattered every time she looked into his liquid dark eyes. But this was so soon for words of love. Victorine looked up, trying to gauge his sincerity.

His eyes met hers without the twinkle of mischief she had glimpsed there earlier. He raised her hand to his lips, kissing her gloved fingers lightly.

"You are so beautiful, little Victorine, that any man would kneel at your feet. I shall need all of my skill as a swordsman to fight off your other suitors."

Her head swam as he kissed her hand, pressing her fingers lightly. She felt a quivering in her stomach, and her heart beat very fast. She had dreamed of this for years, her first romance, her first love, but the reality was more exciting than she had ever imagined. The courtyard around them seemed hazy in the flickering light; if this were a dream, Victorine hoped she would never wake.

And yet, she had been flirted with before. There had been young men in Charleston, at teas and parties, who had also made pretty speeches. How much did his compliments mean? Was Monsieur Valmont in earnest?

André smiled, and Victorine tried to think of a reply. She mustn't let him see that he left her weak.

"Your words are sweet, Monsieur Valmont," she said softly. "Is your heart as true as your words are polished?"

André's dark eyes flashed; Victorine held her breath.

"You doubt my affections? *Mais non*, mademoiselle, you shall see what it is to be courted by André Valmont."

As if his statement alone were not enough to make her breath come fast, he leaned forward. Victorine's eyes widened.

He lifted her hand again and this time turned it to kiss her gloved palm. Even through her thin glove, the warm pressure of his lips made her tremble. His dark lashes were long and thick, and his lips were smooth—how would it be to kiss such a man? It was a daring thought. Victorine shivered again.

"Are you cold?" André asked. "We will go in. But do not forget, my heart is not given lightly, *ma belle*. We will talk of this again. For now, may I have the honor of another dance?"

Victorine nodded. The music drifted out to the courtyard, and she was happy to rejoin the bustle of the crowded ballroom. To sway lightly in André's practiced grasp as he led her through the steps—what bliss.

Was this what marriage to André Valmont would be like—his hand guiding her, his arm always protecting her? Her head whirled at the thought, and her heart seemed to be in her throat.

The music played on, and Victorine floated on a cloud of happiness. She danced with the handsomest man in the room, and he had eyes only for her. She could almost believe that André loved her already, despite the fact that they had just met. The tight bud of excitement inside her blossomed until she felt overcome with happiness. She hoped the night would never end.

Other young men clustered around her, begging for a dance, but she hardly saw them. André alone made the room brighter, the music sweeter.

Later, after André had bowed over her hand one last time and her papa had escorted her and her aunt home, she entered their front door, still feeling dazed.

"Our Victorine was the most beautiful young lady of all," Tante Marie declared fondly.

"Was the ball all you wished?" her father asked.

Victorine nodded, smiling a secret smile. She felt just like Cinderella, except she had not lost her glass slipper, and her happiness had no dark threat to mar it.

Then she remembered the secret ball—and the dark-haired beauty on André's arm who had looked up at him with such trust. For a moment her contentment vanished. Surely André had not whispered the same sweet words to that other girl. Surely, even though he had danced with that dark-haired girl, had smiled and laughed, it meant nothing. A party flirtation, that was all. If he hinted of marriage to Victorine, it must mean that his heart was not engaged elsewhere.

Victorine pushed any doubts away. She had found her prince, and he was as handsome and distinguished as any romantic young lady could wish. Nothing would spoil her newfound happiness.

Nothing!

Chapter 3

The next morning Soozie burst into her mistress's room before Victorine had even opened her eyes. The slave girl called, "Look, mamzelle! This just come for you. 'Tisn't it pretty?"

She held out an armful of scarlet hothouse roses. Blinking sleepily, Victorine could smell the heavy sweet scent from her bed. "Oh yes! Who's it from?"

"A gentleman friend, I bet you." Soozie grinned. "There's a note come with it."

"Oh, give it to me, *s'il vous plaît*." Sitting up in bed, Victorine eagerly accepted the slim missive. Ripping it open, she read quickly:

My dryad,
     The hours are long until I can see you again. Will you have pity on a lovesick heart and allow me to call this afternoon?

Yours with respect,
André Valmont

"Mais oui!" Shrieking, Victorine fell back against her smooth sheets, clutching the note to her heart. She closed her eyes as she savored the delightful anticipation. The special thrill that André's smile evoked, the way her stomach tightened when he touched her hand—she felt almost overcome with these new feelings.

It was more than a brief flirtation, then. Could André truly love her already, after only one night of dancing and conversation? But was that not how love occurred? All the novels and stories seemed to say so. And her own heart sang at the thought of seeing him again.

For a moment she wished intently for her dead mother, for the chance to ask questions that the young Victorine had never thought of. Surely her mother would approve of this courtship by a young man of a good Creole family. Victorine remembered her father's hints about André and his distinguished lineage. And her *maman* had schooled her young daughters in manners and household management, preparing them for marriage and motherhood. That was the sum of a woman's life, Victorine reflected.

Soozie was still watching her curiously. Victorine blushed.

"A young man, I done said it." Her maidservant nodded wisely. "You want me to put these in water?"

Victorine nodded. "I'll arrange them myself presently. Oh, and bring my coffee, please."

Soozie hesitated, looking over her shoulder. "How about some nice hot cocoa again, mamzelle? The coffee's running awful low, and your papa directed Cook to save it for company."

"No coffee?" Victorine looked up in surprise, jarred from her rosy thoughts of André. Perhaps, Victorine thought, the city merchants were not as forthcoming with a slave girl as they would be with the mistress of the house. Her mother had always gone to market with her housekeeper; Victorine had been remiss, lying late in bed her first days home from school. She glanced at the clock on the mantel, then at the pale morning sunlight peeking through her lacy curtains.

"I'll go down to the marketplace with you," she decided. "I'll wear the striped morning dress."

Soozie hurried away with the flowers, then returned to lay out Victorine's clothes and help her with corset lacing and tiny buttons and hooks and eyes.

Within an hour, Victorine had sipped a hasty cup of cocoa and nibbled on a piece of bread and jam. "This bread tastes bad," she objected.

"The flour's no good, Cook says," Soozie explained. "Since the war, nothing be the same."

Victorine shook her head. After consulting with the family cook, a stout gray-haired slave who had known Victorine since she was a baby, Victorine wrapped a warm shawl around her shoulders and tucked a list into her reticule. Then she and Soozie set out for the marketplace, with a basket for their purchases.

She was shocked by what she found, from the half-empty vegetable stalls at the market to the shops on Canal Street. Prices were incredibly high, and the vendors looked glum when she brought out paper money.

"But the banks were asked to switch to Confederate currency," Victorine argued with a woman selling cabbages. "Papa's bank was among the first to issue new paper notes. Don't you support the Southern cause?"

"Causes don't put food in my babe's belly," the woman muttered. She accepted the banknotes reluctantly, then added almost smugly, "Can't give you change. Ain't seen a coin for three days, can't keep them."

Victorine retorted, "Then I'll take an extra cabbage, thank you, to make up the difference." She left the vegetable stall shaking her head.

"We done told you, mamzelle." Soozie hurried after her with the basket only half filled.

"You'd think they would be more patriotic," Victorine complained. "Imagine—not taking the new paper money." She glanced at a nearby stall. "Oh, look. At least there's still plenty of seafood. The Yankees can't keep our fishermen hostage with their silly blockade." She bargained briskly for shrimp and fresh fish, then added her purchases to Soozie's basket.

"Victorine, *mon amie*!" a familiar voice called as they turned away from the fish stall.

Victorine looked up to see Colette waving at her. "Are you better, Colette? I was so sorry that you missed the party."

"My cough is almost gone. Are you done? Come walk with me."

"*Mais oui*. I'm tired of shopping," Victorine admitted. "Soozie, take the basket on home, please."

Nodding, Soozie left with Colette's maid.

Victorine watched the two slaves, heads bent close in conversation as they walked away. She found herself wondering again about the issue that divided the North and South. Why did some Yankees say that slavery was such a bad thing? Her family had always had slaves and had always treated them well. The slaves were protected, her father said, taken care of.

And if some plantation slaves were mistreated, well, that was wickedly unkind, but it seemed so far away from her own life that Victorine seldom thought about it. To fight a war over slavery, over tariffs and states' rights—it was too much for a female brain to understand, her papa said. Victorine knew that she loved her homeland; as for the rest—she'd leave the complicated politics to the men.

Victorine shook the thoughts away and turned back to her friend. They found a vendor selling cups of "Confederate coffee" and tried a cup.

"Pah! What is this?" Victorine made a face. "It doesn't smell like coffee, and it tastes syrupy."

"Probably burnt sweet potato, with some chicory thrown in." Colette shook her head. "New Orleans is not what it was before you went away. How was your shopping?"

"I couldn't believe the prices," Victorine admitted. "Soap is a dollar a bar! Candles are even higher, and I couldn't find any decent flour. What about you?"

Colette unwrapped a parcel carefully. "*Voici.*"

Victorine looked at the leather shoes, puzzled

by her friend's obvious air of triumph. "But Colette, these are boys' shoes!"

"But they fit, and there are no ladies' shoes to be found, not today, at least. The few factories that we have are making shoes for our soldiers, and the ships can't get past the Yankee blockade to bring us lovely wares from France." Sighing, Colette sipped the thick brew.

Victorine sighed. Then she remembered what her afternoon would bring, and she brightened.

"Tell!" Colette had been watching her face. "What secrets are you hiding, eh?"

Victorine blushed. To hide her face, she tried another drink of the counterfeit coffee, then tossed the liquid into the gutter. She handed the thick cup back to the vendor.

Colette followed suit, her curiosity evident. "So?"

"I'm expecting a caller." Victorine lowered her voice and shielded her face with her fan so that no one would overhear. "I met the handsomest young man at the Mardi Gras ball last night—André Valmont."

Colette's smile faded. "Valmont?"

"Papa will be very pleased to hear André is calling; he's most taken with him. Of course, our parents have been friends forever. I think I met him as a child, but I didn't really remember him, not until the ball. Do you know him?"

As she gazed at her friend's face, Victorine felt a moment of panic. *Was Colette in love with André, too? What a quagmire that would be.*

Colette shook her head. "I barely know him. Neither my beauty nor my family's fortune is enough to tempt him."

"Colette!" Victorine exclaimed. "That's most unkind. The Valmonts are rich enough not to care about my wealth. And your beauty is—considerable," she finished loyally. But Victorine didn't meet her old friend's eyes. Colette had thick brown hair that curled nicely. But her hazel eyes were pale and her jaw long, like her late father's.

"And he's so charming—he sent me flowers this morning, and the sweetest note." Victorine forgot her friend for a moment, savoring the memory of André's gallantry.

"Victorine . . ." Colette hesitated.

Victorine raised her brows.

Her friend looked at her for a moment, then shrugged and said, "It sounds like a suitable match."

Victorine plied her fan. "We're not speaking

of marriage, Colette. He's only calling for the first time." Yet that wasn't quite true; André had spoken of his future wife, last night in the courtyard. And her father had dropped broad hints, in his last letter to her at school, of this young man and how eligible he was, how old his family name, how respectable his situation. And of course, she would listen to her papa when it came time to agree to a proposal. What girl would do otherwise?

Yet for an instant Victorine felt uneasy. Her American friends from school, more adamant in their opinions, had seemed shocked that she would allow her father to make a match for her. They believed that women should choose their own husbands; Elizabeth herself had fallen in love with a Yankee soldier, of whom her father did not approve.

But who has my interests more firmly in mind than my own beloved papa? Victorine asked herself stubbornly. *And look at the young man he's chosen —a prince from a fairy tale.*

What could be better than to love André as easily as his good looks and charming manner invited her to do? And to make both their families happy in the bargain?

Despite the war, despite the bare stalls and high prices, life was good.

The two girls chatted as they turned toward home, but Victorine's thoughts had already jumped ahead. What should she wear this afternoon, the blue silk or the pink moiré? And would Cook allow them some of the dwindling supply of real coffee?

Victorine was momentarily distracted by the sight of troops drilling in the square, young men still awkward as they handled their old-fashioned weapons. Some didn't seem to have guns at all, and their marching was ragged.

But if the troops didn't appear practiced yet, it was of little consequence, Victorine decided. She'd heard her papa say that New Orleans had dirt embankments and ditches and two forts to guard the Mississippi River. There was no reason to fear. Victorine hurried home, thinking only of gowns and coffee.

After changing her mind three times, she settled on the pale pink gown, with an overskirt of Belgian lace—elegant, if a little formal for the afternoon. But she wanted to look her best. Soozie helped her dress and redo her hair, and Tante Marie argued with the cook over the matter of the precious coffee.

When the knocker sounded on the heavy front door, Victorine, listening from the upstairs landing, felt her heart pound almost as hard. She fled into the formal sitting room, where Tante Marie had been waiting. This room was reserved for the most important occasions and most distinguished guests.

"Do not allow a gentleman to see that you are agitated," her aunt warned.

Nodding, Victorine seated herself decorously on the settee, arranging her skirts carefully. She picked up her embroidery frame and made small, delicate stitches so that she would not stare eagerly at the doorway.

"Monsieur Valmont to see you, mamzelle," the butler announced.

André came quickly into the room. He made his bow to Tante Marie, then took his time as he bowed over Victorine's hand.

"How nice to see you again." Victorine put down her needlework. She felt her pulse leap, but she tried to look calm. "Joseph, you may bring in a tray. Would you like coffee or wine, monsieur?"

"Wine, s'il vous plaît," André told her.

Both Tante Marie and the butler looked relieved, and the slave withdrew.

Now André had to converse politely with her aunt. Victorine waited impatiently for the two to agree on the weather, the rightness of the war, and the Yankee blockade that cut painfully into the business of New Orleans, the South's greatest port.

Finally André asked a question about her embroidery. "May I?" His attention apparently on the square of fine linen, he crossed the room to sit beside her on the settee, bending closer to examine the tiny stitches. Beneath the cover of the cloth, she felt him caress her fingers. Victorine took a deep breath.

The butler reappeared with a tray, and Tante Marie jumped up to supervise the pouring of the wine. For a moment no one was watching them.

"Ah, my wood nymph," André whispered. "It has seemed an eternity since I saw you last." He kissed her fingers lightly.

Victorine felt a thrill run up her arm and hoped he did not feel her tremble. "You're too kind, sir," she murmured. "It was only last night."

"What does the heart know of time?" With a cautious glance toward her aunt, André moved even closer.

He made a fine picture, Victorine thought, with his starched white cravat and dark blue waistcoat. But his closeness made her both nervous and excited. She was almost glad that her wide skirts forced some distance between them.

"My father may join us soon," she told him. "He often comes up from the bank about this time."

"How nice. I hold your father in great esteem," André told her, his dark eyes gleaming. "But I confess that I would rather devote myself to his lovely daughter."

Victorine held her breath. He said all the right things, but it was proceeding too fast. Courtship was supposed to be a leisurely affair, walks home from church, drives along the river, parties and dinners, eventually the announcement, the engagement breakfast, the planning of the wedding, the setting up of a household. Then she realized that she herself was looking very far ahead, and she felt her cheeks burn.

"Does my presence distress you?"

"Oh no, I mean—" To her relief, Victorine saw that Joseph and Tante Marie had finished pouring the wine and arranging the glasses on the silver tray. Now Joseph offered them both a glass. Grasping the fine crystal stem, Victorine took a sip, glad to drop her eyelids for a moment while she considered what to say to her audacious suitor.

Before she had thought of a witty answer, she heard her father's step on the staircase.

"Ah, André, my boy, good to see you. Marie, *bonjour*. Victorine, *ma petite*, how lovely you look." Monsieur LaGrande kissed his daughter on the forehead, then nodded toward the tray. "A glass for me, Joseph, *s'il vous plaît*."

André would offer no more outrageous compliments with her father so close at hand. Relaxing, Victorine nibbled on a sweet cake and listened as the two men discussed the war.

"I confess I do not like this movement of men to Tennessee," Monsieur LaGrande said. "We need to keep our men here to protect the city. With the Yankee fleet commanded by David Farragut at Ship Island, it seems obvious the Yankees mean to come up the river. This is no time to send our Louisiana troops north."

Victorine felt her eyes widen. A Yankee fleet so close to New Orleans?

"Ah, but we have the great gunboat *Louisiana*," André suggested.

"If it is ever completed." Monsieur LaGrande sipped his wine, his expression grim.

"And the forts on the river—" Victorine added eagerly.

"We still need troops here," Monsieur

LaGrande declared. "And there is a shortage of metal needed to produce cannons. General Beauregard has asked for bells to melt down. The parish churches are already sending theirs in."

As she watched André listening to her father, Victorine's thoughts wandered from the talk of war; she thought instead about André's well-shaped hands and long dark lashes.

An hour later, André glanced at the mantel clock, then stood. "I must go; thank you for your hospitality."

"*Mais non*, it was my pleasure," Victorine said formally.

She blushed again when he bowed over her hand. "Would you and your aunt drive with me tomorrow?" He held her hand for an extra moment; Victorine was very conscious of the slight pressure of his fingers.

"I should be most happy," she said.

"Such a pleasure," Tante Marie agreed.

Victorine watched the fine set of his shoulders as he walked down the staircase. Lost in her own dreams, Victorine jumped when her papa patted her arm.

"So you like this young man, *ma petite?*"

"Oh yes, Papa," Victorine agreed, thinking of the red roses on her bureau, of André's charming words, his handsome smile. "He looks like a prince."

Her father chuckled. "More than that, he is from a fine Creole family. I was concerned that while you were away you might form an unsuitable attachment."

Victorine shook her head. "No, Papa."

"Good. I'm pleased that his courtship is welcomed. I knew you would be a sensible girl and heed your papa's wishes."

Easy enough, when the young man your father selected looked and acted like André Valmont, Victorine told herself.

Why should she wish to risk pain, like her dear friend Elizabeth? After Lieutenant Adam Cranfield had been wounded and captured by Southern forces at the Battle of Manassas, he had been sent back North. Now Elizabeth suffered greatly, wondering where he was.

Victorine's courtship would be different. Even the war could not mar this romance, she promised herself. Love was sweet.

Over the next week, the drives and walks with André continued. When Victorine went with her papa and aunt to mass on Sunday morning, she had much to be thankful for. But as the priest intoned the Latin words, Victorine found it hard to concentrate on the service. Even though André was not in church, the image of his laughing dark eyes lingered.

Trying to shake off her daydreams, Victorine looked around the well-filled church. Many of the churchgoers were Creole families that she knew, but here and there she saw unfamiliar faces. Most of the American settlers were Protestant, but some professed the Catholic faith.

In a front pew she spied a dark blond head, and her brows rose. Surely that man was familiar? As if aware of her gaze, he turned his head slightly and met her eyes. It was the American doctor who had helped her the night of Mardi Gras, when the bully had accosted her in the street.

Recognition leaped in his blue eyes; he smiled directly at her, and Victorine knew that she blushed. She looked quickly down at her gloved hands, clutching her missal tightly. Horrors, did he remember her face? The doctor had been so kind, yet she wanted only to forget that awful night.

For the rest of the long mass, Victorine kept her eyes focused on her lap, hardly daring even to look up at the priest. And when they finally filed out into the square, Victorine was eager to get away and disappear into anonymity once more.

But her father stopped to exchange greetings with another Creole, Tante Marie found a matron to chat with, and Victorine had to wait. Somehow she had half expected the light touch on her elbow. Steeling herself, she turned.

The doctor stood before her, smiling. "Mademoiselle?" Sweeping off his hat, he bowed; she had a moment to look down at his dark blond hair and strong brows. His face was pleasing, if not classically handsome, his nose strong, and his clean-shaven chin jutting, suggesting a strong will beneath his quiet manner.

Then the blue eyes were intent once more on her face. Flustered, Victorine dropped her gaze. He had saved her from disaster; she couldn't just cut him dead. And yet—

"I owe you thanks, I know," she whispered. He leaned closer to hear. "But I cannot—my father—"

"I find myself thinking about you," the doctor said. "I remember your face that night and the scent of your hair, the lilt of your voice with its French accent. It's like hearing a few words of a song, and wishing for more."

Victorine glanced up at him in surprise, saw the honesty in his clear blue eyes, the strength implicit in his broad shoulders. For a moment she felt regret. If she had not already loved André, if the doctor had not been American, and therefore out of the question . . .

"My name is Brent Whitman," he was saying. "Do you suppose your family would allow me to call?"

"Mais non," Victorine heard her father say, his voice stern. "Do you always accost strange women in the street, monsieur? This is not the sign of a gentleman!"

"I meant no offense," Dr. Whitman said quietly, but his tone was steady. "She is not a stranger."

"What do you mean?" Monsieur LaGrande sounded outraged. "Where could you possibly have met my daughter?"

Victorine held her breath, too afraid to speak. She could almost see the shadow of scandal darken the sunlight around them.

Dr. Whitman's expression was rueful. "I meant only that I have seen her at church with her family, and she is . . . difficult to forget." He looked straight at Victorine as he spoke.

Victorine felt such overwhelming relief that her knees trembled. She tried to express her gratitude in one poignant glance before her aunt pulled at her arm, urging her away from this brash American.

"You will not speak to my daughter again, is that clear?" her father was saying.

The doctor bowed gravely, and Victorine did not see his face as her aunt hurried her off.

On the walk home, her father lectured her about avoiding strangers, and Victorine nodded obediently. But despite herself, she couldn't quite forget the young doctor's clear blue eyes and quiet strength.

Chapter 4

"Faster!" Victorine shrieked, waving her handkerchief as the horses pounded past them on the track.

Within moments the horses crossed the finish line. The crowd roared with mingled shouts of joy and dismay. This time Victorine's squeal was lost in the general uproar.

Then she blinked and coughed at the cloud of dust that followed the mass of horses. She covered her nose and mouth with her handkerchief until the dust settled. The handsome young horses with their glossy coats and flashing limbs had made such a fine spectacle. She was so glad that André and his parents had invited her to the Fairgrounds on this beautiful spring day. Laughing a little, she looked up to see André smiling at her.

"You make a fine sportswoman, my dryad. A shame that the racing season has been curtailed, but we must not allow the war to end all our fun, eh?"

Victorine nodded agreement. She still did not believe in any real danger confronting their city, though the Northern forces had maneuvered their fleet to the mouth of the Mississippi River. With the Southern river forts and ships, with all the brave men who marched and drilled in the city and in camps outside—how could the Yankees hope to overcome such loyal Confederates? There had been sad losses to the north, in Tennessee, but the Confederacy was still sure of an ultimate victory.

"Are you having a good time, my dear?" André's mother, Louisa Valmont, asked as she approached, adjusting her parasol.

"*Mais oui*, Madame Valmont. It was most exciting. Thank you for inviting me."

The matron nodded graciously. "I'm so glad you could come. It was a fine race. Now it is time to start back, André."

As they walked toward his carriage, André asked, "Would you like to hear Harry McCarthy at the Academy of Music?"

Victorine looked up eagerly. "The man who performs 'Hurrah for the Bonnie Blue Flag'? I love that song—it's so patriotic. Tomorrow night?"

"No, my little wood nymph. I must see an old college friend tomorrow. But on Friday, eh? We shall take your aunt along to chaperon."

"Of course," Victorine agreed, happy to look forward to another delightful evening. André made every occasion seem special. She had never been so happy. As he handed her into the carriage, she smiled at him again. André tucked a dust robe around her wide skirts, then climbed in and took up the reins.

"Can we go as fast as the horses in the race?" Victorine asked, remembering the fine show as the horses galloped past.

"Not unless you wish to overturn us," André told her, chuckling again. "But we will see what we can do." He cracked his whip, and the handsome pair of bays leaped into action. The carriage jerked; Victorine gasped and held on tight. As their carriage's wheels spun, the vehicle bounced along the rough roadway, coming perilously close to a smaller carriage.

"Here, sir! Curb your horses," the man in the other vehicle called out, frowning.

André slowed the horses to a steady trot. "Satisfied, my dryad? Or shall I tame the wind and ride a cloud for you?"

Victorine returned his smile. "I almost believe you could."

"For you, anything!"

Victorine felt warmed by his love. The sun shone, flowers bloomed, the blue sky was clear. The war seemed far away indeed.

But the next afternoon, when Colette came to fetch her to watch her brother drill, Victorine was abruptly reminded of the civil conflict.

"I thought your brother was still in college," Victorine said, arranging a stylish bonnet on her head.

"The University of Louisiana has closed," Colette told her. "All my brother's friends are signing up. Even my cousin Philippe has joined the Beauregard Cadets."

"What? He's only fourteen!" In front of the looking glass, Victorine paused in dismay.

"It's a cadet troop, only for protection of the city," Colette explained. "I'm sure they won't have to fight. What handsome ribbon. I haven't seen any so bright in the shops."

Victorine smiled as she tied the scarlet bow firmly beneath her chin. "It was a gift from André; I think it came in with a blockade-runner. He said the color suited me."

Colette shook her head. "Has he asked for your hand yet?"

Victorine's smile faded; she stepped away from the glass. "Not yet."

But any day now, she told herself. For weeks André had hinted at marriage, only to shy away before making a formal proposal. Victorine tried not to feel impatient. *He will propose soon, I know it*, she thought. *He loves me, and I love him. Our families approve. What else do we need?*

She and Colette strolled down to the square to watch the parade.

"My brother's troop is all Creole," Colette boasted. "There are so many companies now, all over the city. Some will leave to go North, of course, where the real war is."

"Papa says we need to keep the men here to protect New Orleans," Victorine said, then paused at the sound of martial music. A drummer beat briskly, and the first troop came into view. Cheers rose from the scattered bystanders. Victorine pulled out her handkerchief to wave eagerly.

The members of the first troop that passed wore long-cut dark blue jackets, light blue trousers, and handsome red sashes. The soldiers marched with their shoulders back, heads high.

"Has André signed up yet?" Colette asked.

Victorine bit her lip, her pleasure suddenly

dimmed. "No; he says he can't bear the thought of leaving me."

Colette raised her brows but said nothing.

To distract her friend, Victorine pointed toward the next unit sauntering by. Their bearing was less stiff, and their faces looked dirty and unshaven. "What a fierce bunch."

"That is a Zouave troop—ruffians from the wharves and the jails, I've heard," Colette said, lowering her voice.

The men wore red shirts and short brown jackets with red trim. Their wide-legged trousers were tucked into their boots. Some carried shotguns, others long rifles fixed with bayonets. The man closest to Victorine wore a ragged wide-brimmed straw hat and boasted an ugly scar on his tanned cheek.

Victorine shivered. "These are our defenders?" she murmured to Colette. "I saw Zouave units in Charleston with much more spirit."

But her friend didn't answer; the next unit was her brother's. "*Vive* Gaston," Colette called loudly. Victorine, forgetting her worries, cheered with her.

Gaston grinned at the tribute and almost lost his place in line. He did a quick step to catch up with his fellow militiamen. Both girls watched as the troops marched and wheeled across the square, and the drumbeat echoed in Victorine's ears.

When a cloud veiled the sun, Victorine's first thought was that it would cool the men as they drilled; some were already red-faced and sweating in their wool uniforms. But soon a light spring rain began to fall, and most of the crowd moved on.

Colette exclaimed in annoyance, and they hurried beneath a wrought-iron balcony. Standing within its shelter, Colette turned for a final look at her brother.

A little breathless from her dash out of the wet, Victorine stared across the square where some spectators still lingered. Then she stiffened. That dark-haired young gallant with the pretty girl beside him, surely that was not André?

But she recognized the way he gestured with his free hand, and the slight crook of his lips as he smiled at the girl in the circle of his arm.

Victorine felt a sudden pain in her chest. Who was this girl? She looked vaguely familiar. Not the girl from the ball with whom he'd been dancing? Victorine felt suddenly ill; her stomach churned.

"What is it, *mon amie?*" Colette had noticed her distress. "You're as white as a magnolia blossom."

Victorine couldn't allow her friend to see André with another girl. "I'm overwarm," she said quickly. "Can we go home now?"

"Of course." Colette offered her arm, and they walked home.

Pacing up and down in her room later that afternoon, Victorine fretted over what she had seen. More than a rain cloud had darkened her day. What was André up to? She would demand an explanation as soon as she saw him again— this matter was too delicate to trust to a note. Yet she wanted to know now!

Victorine was happy to be distracted by the butler bearing a travel-stained letter on a silver tray. Victorine snatched it up. "It's from Rosamund," she said aloud. "Oh, *très bien*."

Dear Victorine,

It seems so long since we were together at the Academy with dear Madame and nothing more to worry us than a thorny geometry problem. I miss you and Elizabeth very much; I've had no word of Elizabeth for weeks.

Troubled times, here. My family is almost as disordered as the country itself. My brother Daniel has gone north, not the first Tennessean to don a Federal uniform. He believes in the Union, and he doesn't believe in slavery. My other brother, Tom, supports the Confederate cause. But he's not yet fourteen, too young to fight, and has promised my mother he will not leave us alone on the farm with Pa so ill. Still, he frets when we hear news of the war, and I see him regretting his promise every day.

Now there's been a great battle. You've surely heard of Fort Henry's surrender in February, leaving the Tennessee River an open door to the South. Uncle Tyrone says Governor Harris is a blockhead. The fort was not even finished when the Union gunboats arrived, and our troops carried old-fashioned muskets left over from the War of 1812. Fort Donelson fell next to Grant's Union troops, and we expect Nashville, with its factories and ironworks and stocks of military supplies, will soon be taken. General Grant would accept only an "unconditional surrender." Ma is afraid he is no gentleman, and wonders what will become of Daniel among men like this.

My heart aches over all the bloodshed; black dresses are common now in our neighborhood. My aunt wrote us that when Nashville heard of the surrender, many shops boarded up their windows, and some citizens lined up to buy rail tickets to escape the Yankee troops, "the Blue Hordes." Southern forces are pulling back; worse yet, for us, is that we have had no word of Daniel. I pray every night that he is safe.

God bless you, so far away in New Orleans. Your last letter was so merry; I'm glad that someone has the chance to dance and laugh. Your young man sounds most attentive. I wish you every joy and am only sorry I will not be able to dance at your wedding. Now I must close while I can yet get this letter out.

Your dearest friend,
Rosamund

Victorine wiped her damp eyes and sat down at her dressing table to compose an answer to her friend. She worried about Rosamund's present danger and also about her disgrace in having a brother among the enemy—how could he! Yet was that any worse than Elizabeth's dilemma, falling hopelessly in love with her Yankee officer? Both her friends were to be pitied, Victorine thought. She herself was so fortunate, her home and family safe, André so far spared from the vagaries of war. Victorine told herself she would pray for her friends and give extra thanks for her own blessings.

And Rosamund had no one like André to court her; she sounded lonely and a bit wistful in her letter. Victorine glanced at André's latest floral offering; her room was always scented with his flowers.

Victorine felt almost guilty at her good fortune. True, Farragut's fleet still threatened from the mouth of the Mississippi River, but everyone she talked to said the two river forts would hold them back. New Orleans would never give in!

She wrote for the better part of an hour, then folded her letter and put away her pen. That night she prayed for Rosamund and Elizabeth and for Madame Corday, their teacher who had been so kind to them all, and for their families. After she had read the letter from Rosamund, her troubles with André seemed petty and insignificant. She had many things for which to be grateful.

* * *

When André arrived on Friday to take Victorine and her aunt to the musical program, she made sure that her appearance was pleasing. With Soozie's devoted help, she spent hours arranging her brown ringlets in an appealing cascade that brushed her shoulders. Her dress was a deep midnight blue, trimmed with white lace and jeweled rosettes. Her shoulders were bare, and she wore sparkling sapphire and diamond eardrops and a diamond pendant that her father had given her on her sixteenth birthday.

"You look splendid, child," Tante Marie said with approval.

Surveying herself in the looking glass, Victorine nodded her thanks. She did look every inch a suitable bride for a well-bred Creole gentleman. If André was not impressed, she could do no more. And if his heart was engaged elsewhere —no, she had decided not to consider such a painful thought.

Still, when André arrived and bowed over her hand, Victorine knew that her greeting was more subdued than usual.

André lifted an eyebrow but made no comment as they said good-bye to her father and André escorted the ladies out.

The carriage ride was quiet. Victorine stared at her gloved hands and opened and shut her fan.

Beside her on the narrow seat, André glanced at her, but she did not meet his eyes. He made polite conversation with Tante Marie instead.

When they had entered the Academy of Music and found their place, Tante Marie saw a matron nearby to gossip with. André bent close and said softly, "Are you feeling well, my dryad?"

The playful pet name did not reassure her tonight. Despite her earlier vow to let the matter drop, she found she had to ask him about the dark-haired woman on his arm.

Victorine gathered all her courage. "I—I went this week with my friend to see the troops drill."

"And it distressed you?"

"I thought . . . I thought I saw you there, with a female companion."

Victorine held her breath. For an instant she thought his easy smile stiffened; then he shrugged, his tone unconcerned.

"Did you? I took my young cousin out earlier in the week. My *maman* likes me to do my duty to my family now and then. Perhaps it was that day; I hardly remember."

The relief she felt was immense. A cousin, and André only being his usual charming self. The answer was so simple, and here she had worried for days. She should have known all his family—the Creole community was close-knit—but she had been away, and her earlier memories were vague. Disarmed, she blurted out the other worry that had nagged at the edge of her thoughts.

"And the militia? Will you be signing up soon? All the men are."

This time he did frown. "What, are you tired of my company, little one? Do you wish to send me away, to march up and down like a simpleton and sleep in the mud at Camp Benjamin?"

"Oh no," Victorine hastened to reassure him. "I do not wish you to leave—I am most happy in your company. I only thought—"

"I see no reason to waste my time; I can shoot and ride already, better than those awkward boys in uniform. New Orleans is secure. If the city is threatened, then it will be different. In the meantime, we have our own lives, no? And I would much rather be here with you."

He gave her his most charming smile, and Victorine felt her happiness restored. He did love her; he must. If he put off his patriotic duty to be near her, was it not proof?

She pushed away any lingering doubts. André was brave, she was sure. And if he said there was no imminent danger, why question his judgment?

The heavy velvet curtains parted, and the musical performance began. At first Victorine found herself more absorbed in André's slim strong fingers, which held her hand discreetly. She barely noticed the skits and songs performed by Harry McCarthy, with his Irish accent, assisted by Miss Lottie Estelle.

But when the first notes of McCarthy's most famous number, "Hurrah for the Bonnie Blue Flag," began, Victorine turned her attention to the stage. The tune, she had heard, came from an old Irish song, but McCarthy had written the words specifically for the current conflict.

The singer saluted a flag, brought onto the stage by a young man in a stiff new uniform. Cheers rose from the audience.

With her eyes closed, Victorine listened to the beautiful words that paid tribute to the Southern cause. Her heart swelled with pride as she thought of the young men risking their lives to defend their homes from Northern aggression. And there was her father, pouring the resources of his bank into the struggle, risking his whole fortune. How brave they all were! If only she had been a man and could contribute, too! Like André . . . well, André would fight—hadn't he said so?—as soon as need dictated. But what a grand and glorious cause they were united in!

Victorine also thought of Charleston during the attack on Fort Sumter, where the first guns of the war had been fired. She shivered again at the memory of cannons shaking the schoolhouse, acrid-smelling smoke tainting the air. She had cowered inside the house, but she had been young and foolish. Now she felt much older, more seasoned. She had glimpsed the conflict before anyone else here; she promised herself she would profit by the experience.

As the great Irish singer neared the song's final stanzas, the audience stood and sang along. Victorine jumped to her feet, her voice rising with the others.

> Then here's to our Confederacy; strong we
>   are and brave,
> Like patriots of old we'll fight, our heritage
>   to save;
> And rather than submit to shame, to die
>   we would prefer;
> So cheer for the bonnie blue flag that bears
>   a single star.
>
> Ye men of valor, gather round the banner
>   of the right;
> Texas and fair Louisiana join us in the
>   fight.

Davis, our loved President, and Stephens,
*   statesmen are;*
Now rally round the bonnie blue flag that
*   bears a single star.*

At the mention of Louisiana, the crowd gave a great shout. Victorine clutched André's arm, almost overcome. It was as heady as wine, this feeling of brotherhood, of camaraderie and united purpose. She felt her blood singing in her veins, and she cheered with the rest of the audience.

They were all gathered together in this great crusade; how could they possibly fail? The South would rise together and push back this hateful invasion by men who had once claimed to be their brothers. The South would triumph!

When the song ended, the applause was deafening. Victorine clapped until her hands were numb, and still the uproar continued. One man gave the famous "rebel" yell, which on the battlefield brought fear and confusion to their Northern foes.

"Wa-who-ee!" His raucous shout drew laughter and more applause.

At last André offered her his arm, his dark eyes gleaming with laughter. "I think I must take you away, *ma petite*, before you enlist this very moment."

Reluctantly Victorine nodded, and André ushered them out. But the song's refrain echoed inside Victorine's head as they fought their way through the noisy crowd, and she hummed beneath her breath on the way home.

"Hurrah, hurrah for the bonnie blue flag."

Chapter 5

"There," Victorine said with satisfaction. Ignoring her aching shoulders, she held up a cotton shirt to show Colette and the older ladies who filled the hall. "Another one finished, down to the last stitch."

"Good work, my dear," Madame Hortense told her, her tone approving. "You've both worked very hard today."

"Thank you, madame." Victorine flexed her sore fingers.

"I should say so," Colette added beneath her breath as they put on their shawls and bonnets to leave. "My fingers are about to fall off. I've never sewed for so many hours."

"But just think of all the shirts we can send to our soldiers," Victorine argued. "It's worth our small efforts."

"I'm going down to watch Gaston and his company drill again; can you come?" Colette adjusted her bonnet and veil and pulled on her gloves.

"*Je regrette*. I promised to practice for the charity show to raise money for our troops, and I'm late already. Are you sure you don't want to sing with me?" Victorine asked as they walked out of the building together.

Colette shook her head. "Creating a tableau is fun—it's just posing like figures from a painting—but performing makes me nervous. I'll have enough trouble playing my piano selection; I don't dare sing! Besides, it pleases Gaston when I come to watch."

They parted on the street corner, and Victorine walked on to her rehearsal. After an hour of practice at the rented hall, she arrived home barely in time for dinner.

"Here you are at last, mamzelle," Joseph said as he opened the front door at her knock. "Your papa and aunt are just about to sit down, and Cook is worrying about the soufflé falling."

"I'll be right there, as soon as I take off my bonnet," Victorine promised. She pulled off her headgear, stripped off her gloves, dropped everything on the hall table, then hurried to the dining room.

"There you are, *ma petite*." Her father stood and held out his hand to her.

"I'm sorry to be late, Papa." Victorine lifted her cheek for her father's kiss, then waited for the footman to pull out her chair. She seated herself gracefully, nodding to her aunt, and waited for the servant to ladle soup into her bowl.

"How is your headache, Tante Marie?" she asked politely. Her aunt still looked pale.

"A little better, my child," Tante Marie told her. "I have taken a little tea. I'm sorry I couldn't go with you today."

"And how did the sewing go?" her father asked.

"Very well, Papa. I did two more shirts with my own hands."

"Your efforts are most commendable," her father told her. "I fear we will need all the uniforms we can provide, and there will be more soldiers soon to wear them."

"What do you mean?" Victorine paused, her spoon halfway to her mouth. "Are we not winning the war? The big battle in Tennessee at Shiloh, it was a victory for us, yes?"

"A costly one, I fear; the lists of wounded at the newspaper office are still growing. As a result, the Confederate Congress has passed a conscription act: All able-bodied white male citizens between eighteen and thirty-five shall be inducted into military service for up to three years."

"Three years! Surely the war will not last so long; we've been fighting over a year already." Victorine's hand shook, sprinkling the spotless linen cloth with droplets of soup. *André—would he have to leave right away? Would he be in danger?*

"Oh dear," her aunt murmured.

"It's hard to say how long the war will go on." Monsieur LaGrande shook his head. "But do not allow it to ruin your dinner. We must enjoy this fine food; many of our citizens are having a hard time feeding their families."

He didn't remark on the smaller meals they were all taking, with fewer courses and less extravagant side dishes. Victorine glanced across their own table; she saw more empty tablecloth than ever before.

Abashed, Victorine took another spoonful of soup. Swallowing, she said, "But the free market, Papa; is that not helping the families of the soldiers?"

"Many of the planters are supporting it nobly," he agreed. "Just this week I heard . . ."

Although Victorine listened respectfully, her thoughts flew back to the act of conscription. How soon would André have to go? Her heart ached at the thought of separation, yet she also felt a secret relief.

With so little time left at home, surely he would propose. Perhaps they could even be married before he had to leave. She would finally be sure of his love, satisfied that her strongest feelings were returned. And she would be spared Colette's disapproving looks.

Perhaps her friend did not mean to be wounding, but her constant talk of her brother and her young cousin's drills and uniforms—it reminded Victorine every day that André still wore his usual elegant civilian garb. She herself knew André was patriotic, but what were others —including Papa—thinking of him?

She did not see André that night, but on Friday he came as promised to watch her perform.

The local Creole community had turned out in commendable numbers to support the fundraising effort; ticket money would go to arm and clothe yet another militia unit. Backstage, Victorine waited in the wings until it was time for her first appearance.

She could feel her heart fluttering, and her throat was dry. Would she be able to sing before an audience? But Elizabeth and Rosamund would have said she was brave to try, and this gave her courage. At least the tableaux came first.

The group ahead of her left the stage, wearing laurel wreaths and Grecian robes. The three young women, giggling a little now that their own stage fright had passed, had depicted the Fates, showing their support for the secession.

Now it was time for Victorine. The curtains closed, and she hurried to the center of the stage to take her position. She arranged the skirts of her white dress gracefully around her, touched the blue bunting that adorned her hair, then lifted her arms in the pose she had rehearsed.

The curtains opened once more; she stood very still, her expression as lofty as she could manage, her eyes, she knew, shining with excitement.

"The Spirit of Liberty," Colonel Harriman announced in his loud voice. "To remind us of the noble goal behind our revolution."

Victorine held her pose; applause from the audience was enthusiastic. She remained very still until the curtain closed again, then hurried off to allow two young ladies to get into place for the next scene.

"Lovely, Victorine," Colette whispered.

But her song was still to come. Victorine sipped some water to clear her dry throat, and when the last tableau had been presented, she prepared for the musical part of the program.

First Colette played "Dixie" on the piano that had been pushed onto the stage; then the two du Lac sisters performed on the harp and guitar. At last it was time for Victorine. Still wearing her blue bunting, she stepped onstage. As Madame du Lac touched the keys of the piano, Victorine began her favorite song:

> We are a band of brothers, and native to
>   the soil,
> Fighting for the property we gained by
>   honest toil,
> And when our rights were threatened, the
>   cry rose near and far—

When she reached the refrain, "Hurrah, hurrah, for the bonnie blue flag that bears a single star," the audience whistled and sang and stamped their feet. After the song ended, Victorine curtsied gracefully, as a wave of clapping rolled over her.

When she straightened, a man in the second row caught her eye. It was Dr. Whitman! The tall American clapped heartily, smiling up at her. Victorine blushed and looked away, wishing she had not met his gaze. Her papa would be annoyed if the American spoke to her again. She bowed once more, then ran off the stage while the crowd still cheered.

To her delight, she found André waiting backstage and immediately forgot everything else.

"My dryad, you have brought down the house!" He handed her a thick bundle of red roses and bowed to kiss her hand. Her arms were bare, because of her costume, and the warmth of his touch made her fingers tingle.

"Oh André, did you really like it?"

"You were superb." He guided her off the stage and away from the other performers. They paused in the dimly lit hallway outside. "I will never forget the sight you made; you were a vision of beauty and grace."

Holding the bouquet, Victorine looked up at him. The lingering exhilaration of her successful performance lent her new courage. "Do you mean that, André?"

"Do you doubt me?" He raised his dark brows, but for once she met his gaze squarely. For a moment they stood very close, and neither spoke.

Then André said softly, "I had meant to choose a better place than a dusty hallway, but—" He gripped her hand and dropped to one knee.

Victorine felt her heart thudding almost painfully in her chest.

"My little wood nymph, you are the woman I wish to be my wife, the mother of my children. Will you accept the Valmont name, my protection and eternal devotion?"

The joy that rushed through her seemed to brighten the dim passageway; Victorine felt as if she might soar above the thin carpet, like an angel in flight.

"Oh yes," she whispered. "Yes, André."

"You honor me, my dear." He rose to his feet and bent closer, meeting her lips with his.

Victorine closed her eyes and delighted in the warmth of his touch. His lips were smooth, his kiss sheer delight. All her life Victorine had dreamed of her first kiss—of course it would come from her fiancé.

The sweetness of it made her catch her breath, afraid to break the spell. She could smell a hint of scent, the pomade he wore on his glossy dark hair. His nearness, the feel of his lips against hers, made the blood roar in her ears. She leaned into his embrace, willing him to hold her tighter.

It seemed too soon when he straightened.

"We are crushing your flowers, my dryad. Let us find your father."

"Yes, you must speak to him." Victorine was also reminded of their duties. "And can we be married quickly, before you leave?"

"Leave?" He sounded genuinely puzzled.

"The conscription act, Papa said—"

"Do not distress yourself, my sweet. I have already hired a substitute."

"A substitute?" she repeated, confused.

"The substitution clause, did you not know? Men who cannot or wish not to serve can hire replacements."

Victorine swallowed hard. "But, André—"

"I've hired a poor Irish laborer, not yet eighteen. He's out of work and not due to be conscripted himself for several months. I paid him well, my dear; it will help feed his family while he's away."

"But you do not wish to fight, yourself?" Victorine tried to sort it out.

"If the need arises. But I have responsibilities here," André explained.

"Responsibilities?"

"Should I wish to leave you, just as we are betrothed?"

"Of course not," Victorine said, her voice faint.

He bent to kiss her fingers, and she could not see his expression. Of course he wanted to be with her. Was it not proof of his love?

They retrieved her cloak and joined her father and aunt, both beaming with pride at her performance. Her father's satisfaction was obvious when Victorine told him the news.

"Well done, my children," he said, gripping André's shoulders and bestowing a Gallic kiss on both cheeks. Then Monsieur LaGrande turned to embrace his daughter. "My dear Victorine, your eyes are as bright as the evening star. I know you shall have the happiness you deserve."

"Yes, Papa." She smiled at him.

Tante Marie added her good wishes; then her father hurried them off. As André held her arm, Victorine heard a newsboy in the street. She paused to listen to his call.

"Extra! General Albert Johnston dead at Shiloh."

Victorine caught her breath, and the two men exchanged grave looks. They all returned to the LaGrande home to open a bottle of wine and toast the engagement, but Victorine's joy was now tempered by anxiety. General Johnston was an experienced and skilled soldier; even Victorine could see that his death was a blow to the Confederate cause.

Within an hour André kissed her hand with a great flourish and departed. Her father bade her good-night, and Tante Marie hugged her. Victorine went up the staircase slowly, her thoughts all ajumble. With the general dead, what would happen to the Confederacy? And as for André's hiring a substitute, it was hard not to wonder about his motives. He said he loved the South, but was he willing to prove his devotion?

In her bedroom Soozie helped Victorine undress. The slave girl had already heard the news of the engagement.

"Just think, mamzelle, soon you be a married lady! You going to take me with you? I love babies." She brushed Victorine's hair with short, hasty strokes.

Victorine winced as the brush hit a snarl. "Of course I'll take you with me. You've been with us ever since I was small, Soozie. I will need your help when I have my own house. Who else would I want as my personal maid?"

Soozie beamed. When she had departed, Victorine crawled into bed. But she was too excited to sleep. She tossed restlessly for a time, then sat up again to light her candle and take out a newly arrived letter from Elizabeth. She reread it one more time.

Dear Victorine,

I hope you are well and New Orleans is enduring this conflict. We have had excitement hereabouts—a strange naval battle between two ships covered with iron plates. My brother says this will be the navy of the future. A captured Federal frigate, the *Merrimac*, was rebuilt as a low-riding ironclad renamed the *Virginia*. This amazing vessel destroyed two wooden warships in her first battle, and ran another aground. My father said she would defeat the whole Union navy.

But the Yankees sent an even stranger-looking craft against her, another ironclad called the *Monitor*, which the newspapers said looked like a tin can on a shingle. These two ships pounded each other to a standstill, but my father swears that our valiant *Virginia* has given even President Abraham Lincoln himself some sleepless nights.

At least these naval battles gave me something else to think about, instead of lying awake at night worrying about Adam's fate.

Is your courtship proceeding? I hope you will be happy. I suspect my father of playing matchmaker. He continually brings home young Confederate officers of exceptional breeding; they bore me to tears. He seems to think he can make me forget Adam, as if what I feel for him, though he is a Yankee, and he for me, were only a passing fancy.

My father shall discover he is mistaken. I will find Adam again, somehow, somewhere.

Your friend,
Elizabeth

Victorine put the letter aside and pulled out a sheet of notepaper. She wrote quickly, wishing Elizabeth were there in person. She had been unable to confess her worries about André to Colette. Now, in the letter to her dear friend from school, she poured out her doubts.

Dear Elizabeth,
Tonight André proposed, and I accepted his offer of marriage. I should be very happy, and I am, I think.

I know you can share my joy at my engagement, because you know how marvelous and strange and even fearful it is to love a man for the first time, love him with all your heart.

But sometimes I wonder if he loves me as completely as I love him—because I do, Elizabeth. I love him with every breath I draw, with every waking thought. So I feel doubly wicked to doubt him, to wonder if he loves me truly, and also to doubt his commitment to the Confederate cause. He still has not signed up to fight. If he can't support his own homeland with total devotion, how much love will he be able to offer his wife?

I don't know what to think. But I will try to trust him and be happy. What else can a lady do? If you have any wise counsel, please write.

I hope you are well and have had news of your soldier. I think often of you and your difficult situation.

Your loving friend—

Victorine reread the scrawled lines, then hastily signed her name. She folded the sheet and laid it on her bureau.

Snuffing out the candle, Victorine lay back against the sheets. Trying to recapture her first elation, she stared up at the cream-colored panels above her bed, reliving the thrill of André's kiss.

Only then did she realize that never once had André said "I love you."

Rumors abounded over the next few days—Federal shells set afire barracks at Fort Jackson. Yet it was also said that few men had been wounded or killed, and most of the talk on the street was that the forts would hold out against Yankee invaders.

Victorine continued to go to the sewing society every morning, usually with her aunt, and to bend over her needlework until her back ached and her eyes were weary. It was there one day, amid the chattering ladies, that she received another shock.

She had stopped to stretch and accept a glass of lemonade from a young girl with big dark eyes. She was not quite old enough to let down her skirts and put up her hair, but she looked vaguely familiar. Victorine remarked as much to Colette.

"She's André's cousin, so she'll be your relative soon," her friend informed her, biting off a thread.

Victorine held her breath. "This is his aunt's

child? But he has another cousin, yes? A young woman with dark hair?"

"In addition to Maria, he has three cousins by his mother's sister, whose husband is second cousin to my *maman*, but they are all boys," Colette told her.

"And two babes in arms on his father's side," Tante Marie put in helpfully, "and one woman cousin, already wed with children of her own."

"She has dark hair and a pretty face?" Victorine asked, trying to sound casual.

"*Non*, dark hair, but her nose is as long as a horse's." Tante Marie searched in her apron pocket for her thimble. "But there was a cousin who moved to France . . ." She and Colette proceeded to outline the Valmont family tree.

Victorine hardly heard. This child was not the young woman she had glimpsed with André on the street, and earlier at the Mardi Gras ball. If it was not a cousin, was there another woman in his life? But how could it be, when he had just proposed to her? She thought uneasily of the strange woman Colette's brother-in-law had escorted to the Mardi Gras ball. Surely André could not be as faithless.

Victorine's head spun. She picked up her sewing again, only to lay a half-finished shirt back on the pile moments later. "My head aches so that I can't see," she told Madame Hortense.

"Poor child, you've done too much. Go home and burn some chicken feathers; the smoke always helps my headaches."

"I'll take you home." Tante Marie laid aside her own work.

Victorine nodded, too heartsick to confide her worries. After they had walked home, Victorine went up to her room and tried to nap. But the air in her bedroom seemed heavy and still, and sleep would not come. She ate little at dinner and answered her father briefly when he asked her about her day.

After dinner her father went out to a meeting with other businessmen to discuss the Yankee threat to the city. Tante Marie retired early, her back aching from sewing so long. Victorine was left to sit alone and gaze into her bedroom fire. The swirling flames danced and leaped while she tried to suppress the pain inside her.

Had André lied to her? Did he love someone else? How could she live with the pain, the humiliation? If only she were certain of his love. . . .

A sudden thought came to her, a memory of childhood stories recounting strange goings-on in the slave quarters. It was said that slaves from

Santo Domingo had introduced—or reawakened —the old African religion of *vodu*, or voodoo. Sometimes, it was whispered, white women as well as people of color ventured into the realms of the voodoo queens and witch doctors, and love spells were most often sought after.

To be sure of André's love . . .

This was nonsense, Victorine scolded herself. Her own mother had never subscribed to such pagan ritual. And what their family priest, Father Bartholemew, would say, she shuddered to think.

But the thought would not leave her. To be sure of André's love, to put aside these troublesome doubts, to ensure that Andre looked at no other woman . . .

Hardly believing her own impulse, Victorine jumped up so quickly that her corset stays pinched. She caught her breath, then called, "Soozie, bring my cloak!"

When she whispered her intention into her maid's ear, the slave's eyes widened. "The voodoo? Oh no, mamzelle, you don't want them— they's wicked, read your mind, they do! Might put a bad spell on you."

"I'll pay them well not to," Victorine said firmly, trying to sound brave. "I want you to take me to see a voodoo queen. I know you know about such things."

Soozie tried to dissuade her, but within half an hour they had slipped out of the house to walk along a dark street, winding their way into a poor section of New Orleans that Victorine had not seen before.

The streets were dark and deserted. Victorine thought of her last illicit adventure and prayed fervently that no one would accost her again. Yet what right had she to pray while she sought such unholy aid?

When they reached the small cottage, Soozie nodded to her mistress to knock.

Her knees suddenly weak, Victorine tapped lightly on the wooden door. She almost hoped no one would answer so that she could turn her back on this small dark house and hurry home.

But a voice called, "Bring yourself in."

Taking a deep breath, Victorine pushed the door open and stepped inside. Soozie, her hands clutched tightly together and her expression anxious, hesitated just outside the door.

The dark-skinned woman who sat in the tall carved chair seemed to loom out of the shadows. Her black dress was hung about with glass beads and charms. She had masses of dark hair tied into strange-looking knots, and a beaklike nose. Her eyes held power and her tone was commanding.

"Sit down, child." She motioned to a rough stool. "What you want from me?"

Victorine, who had never taken an order from a person of color in all her life, sank without question to the low seat. Too late, she saw that looking up to this strange personage only enhanced the voodoo queen's air of authority. Her heart beating quickly, Victorine had to steady her voice before she spoke.

But the black woman answered her own question. "An affair of the heart, eh?"

Victorine gulped and nodded, her mouth dry. Could this strange woman really read her mind?

"You want power to put the spell on your man? Is it the dance you want? To drink the blood and worship the snake, and whirl the night away with brothers and sisters of the faith?"

Victorine couldn't breathe. Shadows at the edge of her vision wavered and seemed to grow, as if the darkness were reaching out for her. With great difficulty she forced her head to move, shook it from side to side. But she felt heavy all over, weighted down, as if enmeshed in an iron net.

The voodoo queen looked amused. "A *gris-gris* then; you want a charm, missy?"

Victorine tried to find her voice; it sounded

rusty and hoarse. "I just want him to love me," she whispered.

"Oh, he going to love you, child. He worship at your feet and never look at no more women. My *gris-gris* are the strongest in the city—don't no one doubt it." She reached into a roughly carved wooden box by her side and took out a tiny packet of powder. "Put this into his wine."

When the woman named the price, Victorine gulped, but she dug into her reticule.

Scooping up the money, the voodoo queen eyed Victorine's little bag hungrily. "And I got a stronger charm—black cat bones—skinned him with my teeth, I did. Buy this one, and it'll make the man your slave."

This time Victorine shook her head, trying not to shiver. She reached for the powder tied up in coarse cloth, almost afraid to touch it, and tucked it into her bag.

"Thank you," she murmured, and stood up.

The woman peered at her through the shadows. "You want more spells, you come to me, eh? I got powers of life and death, child. You remember."

Victorine did tremble then, and the voodoo queen cackled with laughter.

Victorine ran out of the cottage. Soozie, her eyes frightened, waited at the gate. As they hurried down the muddy street, Victorine seemed to hear echoes of that ungodly laughter all the way home. But she clutched her bag tightly, with its packet of love powder. She would put it into André's wineglass the next time he came, and her worries would be over.

But when she climbed into bed, she felt less confident. What if the powder was poison instead? Who could trust a voodoo queen? And even if the love potion did hold all the power the queen had claimed, what had Victorine gained? If André's love could be obtained only through a spell, how much was it worth?

Victorine lay awake all night. When dawn streaked the sky through her windows, she rose and went to her reticule. Taking out the packet of powder and throwing a shawl over her nightdress, she crept quietly down the stairs and out to the farthest end of the courtyard. Beneath a tall banana tree, she shook the cloth free of its white powder, grinding the stuff into the dirt with the toe of her slipper.

So much for *gris-gris* and the powers of voodoo. Today she would go to church and ask the priest for confession. She would likely be given so many prayers of contrition that her knees would be blue. But tonight she would be able to sleep again, knowing that her mother did not look down from heaven and sorrow for her daughter's sins.

And André would love her from his own heart, or not at all.

Chapter 6

On the morning of Good Friday, April 18, Victorine walked slowly to the cathedral, her father and aunt beside her, Soozie and several other household slaves a few paces behind. The city was hushed on this holy day, cries of street vendors muted.

Inside, the church was filled with worshipers. Victorine saw Madame Valmont across the aisle, but André was not in the pew. And toward the back, was that Dr. Whitman? The American did not seem to see her, and Victorine looked quickly away, feeling guilty about her eagerness to steal a glance at him.

Victorine followed her father to their usual pew and knelt beside him. She had rehearsed a list of the people she must pray for, her mother and little sister always topping the list. She also prayed for her city. "God keep us safe from the Yankees," she murmured, gripping her hands tightly together, then added a fervent plea: "And let André love me, and only me!"

When they came out, the courtyard was filled with small knots of people. Her father paused to speak to an acquaintance, and Victorine heard the anxious voices around her.

"The Federal gunboats are shelling the river forts; it's a terrible bombardment. The barracks at the fort are on fire again," a stout man said, his face flushed.

"Our big gunships are still not completed— they were to have been our salvation, destroying the blockade," another man added, his tone anxious.

"What can General Lovell have been thinking of?" a gray-haired gentleman demanded, thumping his gold-headed cane against the paving stones.

"It's not his fault," Monsieur LaGrande argued. "What about the navy?"

Cold with fear, Victorine tried not to listen. *How could the Federal forces have come so close, to be virtually on the city's doorstep? Why was the Confederacy not better prepared?*

When her father offered her his arm again, Victorine was eager to hurry home, to climb the stairs to her bedroom and try to forget what was happening outside. From her bureau she picked up the silver-framed miniature of her mother. She sank onto a low chair, pushed down her billowing skirts, and held the small picture close to her heart.

"Oh, Maman," she whispered, "look down from heaven and protect us; I am so afraid."

She went to bed early, unable to choke down more than a bite of dinner, yet slept little. She dropped into a restless sleep just before dawn but woke shortly after, from a dream of Charleston schooldays and the attack on Fort Sumter. She could hear the cannons again, feel the building shaking beneath her, smell the acrid scent of gunpowder.

Victorine slid out of bed and hurried to open the shutters at her windows. Leaning out over the quiet city, hushed in the early morning, she could hear it clearly—the distant booming of guns. The Yankees continued to shell the forts, and the forts fired back at the Federal ships coming up the Mississippi. If the forts fell, those ships would steam on to New Orleans.

Shivering, Victorine banged the shutters shut again. She hurried back to bed, pulling the sheet up over her head. Still the faint echo of guns crept through the louvers, and even in her own room she did not feel safe. When she finally went downstairs, she found the dining room empty.

"Where's Papa?" she asked the butler, who quickly poured her a hot cup of tea.

"Gone down to the newspaper office, mamzelle, to see if they's any news about the forts. And Mamzelle Marie is in bed with a sick headache."

Victorine sipped the weak tea, thinking wistfully of her prewar coffee, but she couldn't eat the bread and butter on her plate. Pushing it away, she wandered up to the sitting room to pace up and down, listening for the faint boom of far-off cannons. Just when she thought her frayed nerves could bear the suspense no longer, the butler appeared in the doorway.

"Monsieur André, mamzelle."

Victorine rushed to the parlor, holding out both hands. "Oh, André, this is so dreadful! What if the forts fall? What will happen to our city?"

"Hush now, my dryad, you must not be faint-hearted." André kissed her forehead. He motioned for her to sit, then took his place beside her.

Victorine clung to him. The present crisis made her earlier anxieties about her fiancé seem less important. All she could think of today was the city's danger. "But—"

"The forts will not fall. And besides, there is

a barricade across the river, schooners linked together with great iron chains; the Federal ships cannot cross without ramming them or fouling their propellers in the lines. Also, fire rafts are ready upstream."

"Fire rafts?" Victorine tried to steady her voice.

"Our men will set them afire and let them float down amid the Federal navy, catching the wooden ships afire. If the enemy vessels try to evade the fires, they'll likely ram each other or go aground."

Victorine nodded hopefully.

"And"—André lowered his voice, as if a Yankee spy might be hiding behind the settee— "we have the ram *Manassas*, which they call the Turtle. The *Manassas* can knock a hole into the side of the biggest ship, disabling it almost at once. Didn't it drive the Federals out of the river last October?"

Victorine nodded.

"And finally, we have the two great gunships," André went on. "They say the *Mississippi* alone will break the blockade in weeks; nothing the Yankees have will be able to stand up to it."

"But it's not finished!" Victorine wailed. "I heard Papa and his friends discussing it after mass yesterday."

"It will be soon." André patted her hand. "Do not distress yourself. All will be well, you will see."

Soothed by his confidence, Victorine was able to join him when the butler brought in a tray of tea and small cakes. It was the first food she'd eaten all day, and she discovered she was ravenous—no wonder her knees had been weak.

When Monsieur LaGrande joined them, he brought several newspapers. While Victorine poured her father a cup of tea, he read aloud the journals' remarks.

"The *Bee* says there is 'no cause for such a high degree of anxiety.' The *Delta* admits that the city is in 'serious peril,' tells us the defense of the river is 'paramount,' and urges the city not to give credence to 'excited rumors.'"

"If only the gunships were completed," Victorine murmured, passing the plate of cakes, "I would feel more secure."

"So should we all," Monsieur LaGrande stated grimly. "Our present navy is a hodgepodge affair." He waved the food away after André helped himself to another cake. "New Orleans prepared itself for a land attack, and we find ourselves vulnerable from the river, which has always been our biggest highway—ironic, no?"

Victorine wanted to stamp her feet. "These generals, they are *imbéciles*!"

Monsieur LaGrande shrugged. "I've heard that Lovell did ask for the command of the naval forces, but it was denied him—too much bickering among our own forces, I fear. The navy doesn't answer to the army, and the River Defense Fleet doesn't answer to anyone. I pray the city does not suffer because of it."

His tone was somber. It was back again, the heavy weight of fear that made her throat close up and her stomach knot. Victorine swallowed hard. But this was Holy Week; tomorrow was Easter Sunday. Surely, as the priests and ministers had all declared, God was on their side. Surely He would not allow New Orleans, the South's greatest banking and commercial center, the gateway to the whole Mississippi Valley, to fall?

While the two men talked, Victorine stirred her cooling tea and tried to prevent the cup from rattling in its china saucer.

Victorine woke early on Easter Sunday, but her first thought was of the battle. Were the forts still holding? She dressed for mass with shaking hands, then was glad to have Soozie take over, fastening her buttons and pinning up her thick hair. But Soozie trembled, too, and dropped the hairbrush.

"Mamzelle, you think those Yankees will shoot us all?"

"Of course not." Victorine tried to sound confident, but her stomach was still knotted from her own anxiety. Her toilette finished, she hurried downstairs. Her father and her aunt waited in the front hall.

"Any news of the forts?" Victorine asked.

Monsieur LaGrande shook his head. Tante Marie looked white and drawn, but she gave Victorine a nervous smile.

They made their way to church without talking. The streets were crowded despite the early hour, and the murmurs were all of the battle—how did it go? Did the forts hold?

Victorine prayed even harder for the city's safety. But somehow the service failed to penetrate the fog of anxiety that surrounded her. She felt even more worried when they sat down later to an Easter dinner.

"Try to eat," her aunt urged.

"My dear, you must not distress yourself," her father agreed when he saw her untouched plate. "I will tell you"—he leaned toward her and lowered his voice as the butler went out of the room —"and you must not repeat this. I had it from a friend in position to know. The *Louisiana* has been moved down the river just above the forts."

"One of our gunboats is finished, then?" Her spirits rising, Victorine smiled in relief. Her worst fears of Yankee troops surging through the city, taking away André and her father, leaving her defenseless and alone—these were only nightmares, to be dispelled by the rational light of day?

"Unfortunately, no, it has no power, but the large guns are working, and they may be needed. So we have some use of it, and the *Mississippi* will be finished in two more weeks. You must not worry so."

He patted her hand, and Victorine nodded. Her papa was always right. She picked up her fork, determined to have faith.

But it was hard to remain confident as rumors flew through the city over the next few days. The Yankees were plotting to burn the city; the Yankees were giving up and sailing back down the river; the Yankees were marching overland to surround the forts; the Yankees . . .

"Are likely to take wings and fly if we believe everything we hear," Victorine said defiantly to André, determined not to allow herself to fall into despair again. Tante Marie, sitting on the other side of the family parlor, tittered, her laughter nervous and high-pitched.

André looked up from a newspaper as Victorine poured a cup of tea. "The *Crescent* says that New Orleans cannot be captured for at least six months, and within a month, Bronze John will return and prove even more disastrous to our Northern foes than our guns." He accepted the tea with a reassuring smile.

Victorine shuddered at André's mention of Bronze John, or yellow fever. From the loss of her mother, she knew personally how fearsome the disease could be. She didn't wish that fate upon anyone—even their Yankee enemies.

"The city will hold out," Victorine said, to herself as much as to André. "We will not give in."

She was determined to return to her usual routine. She would not cower at home any longer; she must show her faith in the Confederate forces. So on Thursday morning, April 24, she set out for the market, with Soozie at her elbow carrying a basket.

Victorine was inspecting some fresh fish when a small boy ran into the store, shouting, "The Federals have passed the forts! They're approaching the city!"

"No!" Victorine protested. "It can't be true."

But shoppers and shopkeeper alike rushed into the street, their voices rising in fear and anger. Then a loud clear peal cut through the chatter. Victorine thought her heart might stop. It was the bells of Christ Church on Canal Street, and she held her breath to count the number of strokes—one, two, three . . .

When she had counted twelve, the bells ceased; then other church bells around the city repeated the awful message. Twelve peals was the alarm signal, the sign for all the local militia units to rush to their headquarters and arm themselves for battle.

It was true, then; the Yankees were coming. The city was in terrible danger.

The portly fishmonger pulled his shutters shut and banged his door closed. Other shopkeepers were following his example, as anxious shoppers milled in the street.

Victorine shook with fear. "We must go home," she told Soozie, though their basket was only half full. The slave girl nodded.

Victorine pushed her way through the crowd in the streets as the scene became more and more confused. She saw students pouring out of a local day school, dismissed to go home, their expressions mirroring fear and wild excitement. A streetcar stood uselessly in the middle of the street, its horses being led away by a man in uniform who had commandeered the animals for other duties. Women stood on street corners and wept, while in the squares youthful soldiers were packing up tents and forming uneven lines.

At home Victorine found her aunt in tears. Pausing a moment to pat the older woman on the back, she called to the butler, "Bring Tante Marie a glass of wine."

Then Victorine hurried through the house, looking for her father. But he must still be at the bank, or at the newspaper office in search of up-to-date bulletins. The household slaves looked agitated; the butler's collar was unfastened when he brought the wine, and Soozie jumped every time Victorine spoke.

She sat down to write a note to André but tore up the half-written message. Impulsively Victorine picked up her bonnet and called for Soozie.

"Oh, mamzelle, you don't want to go out there!"

"I can't stand waiting; I must know what's happening," Victorine told her maid. "Come, we won't stay long. Don't tell my aunt; she's lying down in her room."

The confusion outside was even greater now than earlier in the day, as was the size of the crowd on the street. No one seemed to know what was happening, but Victorine heard several citizens talk of the wharf, and she headed for the riverfront.

She saw drayloads of cotton being rushed to the wharves as she made her way down the muddy streets, catching the feeling of urgency that now swept through the city. Beside the river were great stacks of cotton bales, bags of corn and sugar and rice.

"What are you doing?" she called to a man who heaved a heavy bundle, his sweat-soaked shirt sticking to his back.

"We can't leave it for the Yankees!" he shouted to her. "We're going to burn the cotton."

"Burn the cotton?" Victorine blinked in surprise, then felt her eyes dampen as she understood these desperate actions. Cotton was the cash crop of the Deep South, the source of New Orleans's wealth as it was bought and sold and shipped to European markets to be made into cloth.

It seemed right. If they could not hold their city, this coarse white "gold" would not fall into enemy hands, would not enrich the Yankees or clothe Union soldiers.

She held her breath as the man splashed kerosene over the stacked bales, then tossed a flaming brand into the heart of the cotton. A tongue of fire leaped up, hesitated, then grew larger.

A whiff of smoke made Victorine cough and move back a little. She walked slowly along the riverfront. She saw that they were burning not only warehouses full of cotton but also those stacked with food. She couldn't help thinking how useful those supplies would be to the city's poor, already hard-pressed to keep their families fed, with so many men gone to fight.

Obviously others had had the same thought. Women in threadbare aprons were fighting their way through the crowd to take away sacks of rice or sugar or corn. Men and women and even children pushed and shouted and struggled to save some of the bounty going up in smoke, but despite the unorganized and impulsive looting, most of the supplies burned.

A hogshead of molasses had been dropped in the confusion, and molasses flowed slowly down the gutters in the street. Victorine had to lift her skirts to jump over the thick dark liquid.

She saw two boys struggling to roll a barrel over the cobblestones and a man going by with a wheelbarrow full of sacks. A stout woman puffed her way down the street, a small child under one arm and a smoked ham under the other.

"At least our enemies will not feast on our

stores," Victorine murmured, trying to comfort herself.

The shouts of the crowd grew louder, the people's expressions more frenzied. Their mood and lack of control were frightening. Victorine felt small and alone in the milling mob.

"Mamzelle, can't we go home now?" Soozie pleaded.

Victorine nodded. The smoke and heat were becoming oppressive, and her whole body was sore from being pushed and shoved. But at least this time, unlike the day when Fort Sumter had fallen, Victorine had braved the chaos, not cowered inside.

Then, out of the crowd, a familiar face caught her eye. Victorine blushed and looked away. But he had seen her.

The tall American pushed his way through the mob, took her arm, and helped her away from the crush. "Are you all right?" Dr. Whitman asked, his tone concerned. "What are you doing here?"

"I wanted to see what was happening," Victorine tried to explain. "I'm on my way home now."

"It's best," he agreed. "May I escort you?"

Victorine felt disloyal. "I have a fiancé, André Valmont," she said quietly. "He will protect me. But thank you."

"He is a fortunate man." Dr. Whitman bowed slightly and released his hold on her arm. "I would advise you to get off the streets quickly."

"I will." Victorine gave him a brief smile, then turned away. She and Soozie walked rapidly. The streets were full of soldiers, grim and quiet as they marched—where? Was the army pulling out of New Orleans? Who would fight for the city? Victorine wished she had asked Dr. Whitman.

When they reached home Victorine had to knock twice before the butler opened the door. She asked quickly, "Is Papa here?"

The butler's face was gray with fear. "Yes, mamzelle. In the parlor."

Victorine dropped her bonnet and gloves on the hall table and hurried up the stairs. She found her father looking out the tall windows with their wrought-iron railings, watching the heavy columns of black smoke that rose from the riverfront. It looked as if the whole city were afire. Her aunt sobbed quietly, her shoulders hunched as she shrank into one of the horsehair-covered chairs.

"Papa, what about the gunboats? Is the *Mississippi* finished?"

His expression told her the answer. "They've ordered it burned, to keep the Yankees from seizing it and using it against us."

It was too much. Their last hope, gone. Victorine sank onto the settee, her knees weak. Her father's face was set in grim lines; he looked as if he had aged ten years in a day. She wanted to weep like a child.

"But the army—will they not fight?"

He shook his head. "Militia with shotguns are no match for powerful gunboats. The Federal navy will float high on the river, their heavy guns looking down on a city full of women and children. How could we risk it?"

For a moment Victorine's outrage overcame her fear. "We must fight, we must! We cannot give in so tamely."

Her father's shoulders sagged. "It cannot be done, *ma petite. Je regrette.*"

She ran to him and put her arms around his neck, and they clung together. Through the windows the heavy columns of smoke continued to rise, as New Orleans burned its lifeblood.

What would happen to their city now?

Chapter 7

Victorine woke late Friday morning after a restless night. Her first thought was of the battle; where were the Yankees? She rushed to the window, opening the shutters to see thick columns of black smoke still rising from the riverfront.

How were Colette and her family faring? Victorine wished she could speak to her friend, but Colette probably had her hands full with her widowed mother and the younger children.

Victorine also thought of Elizabeth, far away in Virginia. Elizabeth had witnessed the conflict firsthand. What would she say of the Yankees' approach?

Victorine found a sheet of paper and pulled her inkwell closer. She wrote quickly.

Dear Elizabeth,
The Federal gunships have passed the river forts and come ever closer; I have such fear of what they may do to my be-

loved city. Papa says we have no way to resist. He is not of an age to fight, but the young men, my André, boys like Philippe, my friend's cousin—what will become of them? Will they be killed or imprisoned?

I wish you were here to tell me that not all Yankees are animals, that they will have some respect for our homes, will not murder or loot. I am so afraid!

Her hand trembled, and she saw that she had blotted her page. She pushed the letter away. She would finish it later.

She rang the bell for Soozie and was pulling on a cotton day dress by the time her maid appeared with a cup of tepid tea.

"Mamzelle, you're not going out there?" Soozie pleaded. "Your papa—he won't allow it. It ain't safe."

"Don't you tell him then," Victorine said firmly. "I have to see what's happening."

Within minutes her hair was hastily pinned up, the veil of her bonnet pulled over her face, and a shawl thrown around her shoulders. Victorine tiptoed down the stairwell, a reluctant Soozie behind her, and slipped out of the house.

It was only a few blocks to the riverfront.

Victorine found the streets still filled with people. Today the mood of the crowd seemed even darker and angrier than the day before. At the riverfront thick columns of smoke still hung in the heavy, moist air as warehouses and ships and smoldering cotton continued to burn. Victorine struggled to breathe.

Then, through the smoke, she saw it—the dark, ghostly silhouette of a ship. Men thronged the sides and hung on the masts. A Federal gunship, filled with troops—it was true, then; the city was indeed lost.

Victorine felt tears rolling down her smoke-darkened cheeks. When she tried to wipe them away, her fingers were blackened with soot. She sobbed aloud, watching David Farragut's Federal navy approaching to lay claim to the South's greatest port, the city that was never supposed to fall.

The crowd murmured, then shouted in anger. The sound made her think of wild beasts at bay. She had never seen a mob of such uncertain temper. The tension was thick; it filled the air like the moisture that rose from the river.

Soozie plucked at her sleeve. "Please, mamzelle, we best go home now."

Victorine nodded. She had no heart to watch their enemies take their first steps onto New Orleans's soil. Heartsick, she pushed her way out of the crowd and turned back toward home, arriving just as a heavy rain began to fall. "Even the heavens are weeping," Victorine murmured.

Fortunately her father had gone out, but Tante Marie was close to hysterics, meeting them at the front door before Victorine could even take off her bonnet.

"*Moi*, I told your papa you were still abed, and when I went to check on you—nothing! Have you no fear, my child?"

"I'm all right, Tante Marie." Victorine patted the older lady's shoulder. "Do not upset yourself."

"Then hurry and pack." Her aunt had already turned back to the staircase. "We must leave for the country before the enemy takes control of the town. Who knows what they will do? They are no gentlemen, these Northerners! Your papa wants us packed by the time of his return."

Victorine shook her head. She was afraid of what lay ahead, but she had no intention of leaving her home.

She climbed the stairway slowly to her room and sat down to finish her letter to Elizabeth and begin one to Rosamund. She would give much to see her friends now, to hear their voices, feel a reassuring hug. She remembered the Christmas

Eve the three of them had clung together, shedding tears of homesickness, and how later, when war had come, the turmoil had been easier to face together. Elizabeth and Rosamund were always brave, and now Victorine knew that she herself had changed greatly over the past year. The pampered girl who had attended Madame Corday's Academy for Young Ladies had been left behind. This time she would behave with more dignity. She added to her letter to Elizabeth:

The Yankee ships are indeed here. I have seen them with my own eyes, eyes wet with tears. And our city has fallen with little resistance. I am ashamed for our citizens, and for all our Confederate leaders who did not foresee the threat from the sea. What lies before us now I do not know. My papa wants to send me into the country, but I intend to stay and face our enemies. You would not run away; this time, neither will I.

She heard quick steps on the staircase, and her father rushed into her room.

"Victorine, why are you not packed? Your aunt leaves within the hour, before the Yankees post guards around the city. You must go to your uncle's plantation. You will be safe there."

Victorine took a deep breath. She had never crossed her father before, never dared to disagree. A good Creole daughter always obeyed her father's commands, and later her husband's. Thus her gentle mother had done, and Victorine had never thought to do otherwise. But never before had Victorine confronted war.

"I will not run away," she said, her voice low but steady. "This is my city, my home."

"I can hardly believe my ears!" Monsieur LaGrande seemed as much astonished as angry. "Victorine, *ma petite*, have you taken leave of your senses? It is not for you to say; I have decided!"

She shook her head, finding it hard to meet his eyes.

"Soozie will pack your trunk; a carriage has been ordered. The train cars are filled with soldiers moving out."

"You may send my trunk if you wish, Papa, but I am not leaving."

"Victorine! How can you disobey your own father?" This time he did raise his voice. "I should never have sent you away to Charleston. This disobedience does not come from your early schooling at the convent, but from wicked American ways."

Victorine trembled, but she lifted her chin. "Papa, I must support the cause I believe in, just as the soldiers do. I would gladly give my life for the Confederate cause. I cannot shoot a gun, but I can at least stand fast on my native soil. Do not take this away from me; I beg you."

"Sewing uniforms, rolling lint, and making bandages are suitable ways for a female to aid the war effort." Her father lowered his voice again, to her relief. "Your loyalty is commendable, but your opinions must not lead you into disobedience to your papa. This is not right."

"I'm sorry if it angers you, Papa, but I am not going." This time she met his eyes and did not look down.

Her father threw up his hands in frustration. "*Mon Dieu*, the whole world is going mad!" He stamped out of her bedroom.

Her knees weak, Victorine sank down on a low chair. When her aunt arrived to continue the argument, Victorine listened to her politely, then kissed her on the cheek.

"I'm sorry, Tante Marie. I cannot go."

"But how can I leave you, child?" Her aunt wrung her hands, her face pale.

"Go," Victorine told her. "My uncle will

need you more, with his wife in the family way. I shall be safe with Papa."

Tante Marie wept, but Victorine, having faced down her father, would not give in now. She saw her aunt off, the older woman's traveling bonnet untied, strings flapping about her face.

As Victorine waved good-bye, she thought about André. Would he have gone to the army? Would he come first to say good-bye?

Scarcely had her aunt been driven away in the old-fashioned carriage when Colette appeared, looking agitated.

"Colette! Come in. Any news?"

"The Yankees have sent two men to City Hall to demand the surrender of the city. Our neighbor says the crowd was so wild he thought the two would be lynched! It's awful, Victorine. Maman and I and the children are leaving for our house in Baton Rouge. Will you come with us?"

This time Victorine felt only gratitude. She hugged her friend fiercely, then shook her head. "I am staying."

"But why?" Colette looked bewildered. "What good can you do here?"

"I don't know," Victorine told her honestly. "I just know I cannot run away."

"But your papa—"

"Is angry at me, I fear." Victorine smiled ruefully.

Colette looked at her with new respect. "I think you are mad, but also brave, *mon amie*. If you change your mind, you are always welcome."

"Thank you," Victorine told her. "I will remember."

"And André—what does he do?" Colette asked.

Victorine felt a tremor of uncertainty. "I haven't heard," she admitted. "No doubt he will join the army now."

"Perhaps, perhaps not," Colette said, not quite meeting her friend's eyes.

"What is it? What do you know?" Victorine grabbed her friend's arm, giving her a shake. "It's about André?"

Colette hesitated. "I think you should be told." She looked at the door, and Victorine hurried to shut it so that no one would overhear. "Perhaps I ought not tell you, Victorine. Maman says women should not know of these things and should pretend not to know if they do. She says my sister is very foolish to weep and carry on; it's only the way men are."

Victorine felt bewildered. "What do you mean?"

121

"Remember the masked ball I dragged you to, during Mardi Gras?"

Victorine nodded, still confused.

"It was an octoroon ball, and those women—they were women of color, descendants of slaves."

"*C'est impossible*," Victorine protested. "The ladies, they were no darker-skinned than you or I!"

Colette's tone was glum. "*Mais oui*. It is true. They have more European blood than African, after generations of these alliances. But the law still forbids marriage between a white and a person of color. Otherwise, my brother-in-law would never have courted my sister. I do not wish you to be so unhappy."

"But André would not—"

"He already does," Colette interrupted. "He has a woman set up in a little house on the same street as my brother-in-law's establishment. I saw him when my sister and I spied on Pierre."

She pushed a slip of paper into Victorine's suddenly cold hand. "There are the directions, if you choose to know."

Victorine felt her head spinning, confused by sordid complications she'd never suspected.

"I'm sorry, *mon amie*. Do not hate me for telling you." Colette sounded anxious. "I must go. If you change your mind about Baton Rouge, come to us."

Victorine nodded, still mute with shock. She hugged Colette once more, then sat back as her friend hurried away. It could not be true; André must love *her*. Had he not proposed? She felt his betrayal like a physical pain; how could she love him so much and he not return her love? She took a deep breath, trying to make the hollowness in her chest go away. *Oh, André.*

But Victorine had seen the two together with her own eyes, once at the masked ball and once on the street corner. André had lied to her when she asked him about the woman, and with the confusion of war, she had been too distracted to confront him again. Perhaps she was afraid to hear his answer.

Victorine put her head in her hands and sobbed aloud. She had seen André leaning close to the other young woman, smiling into her eyes —this hateful thief who had stolen André's affections.

Jumping up, Victorine paced restlessly. She refused to accept what Colette's *maman* had said. Why must it be this way? Why must good wives relinquish their husband's love and loyalty?

This was a more personal threat than even

the Yankees with their armies and ships. And she would fight back. She would find this hussy and tell her that André Valmont had room for only one woman in his life.

And Victorine meant to be that woman.

Chapter 8

The next morning Victorine woke to a clatter of broken dishes. When she went to see what was wrong, she found that the footman had dropped a tray in the hall, shattering the china. Sighing, she returned to her room to dress.

The atmosphere in the LaGrande household was still tense, and the whole city remained in an uproar while negotiations between the mayor of New Orleans and David Farragut continued. Everyone's nerves were frayed.

When Soozie brought Victorine a light breakfast on a tray, Victorine wondered what the slaves were thinking. How did they feel about the prospect of Yankee conquest? It could mean their freedom.

"Soozie, are you happy here?" Victorine asked abruptly.

"Oh, yes, mamzelle. This be my home," the slave girl assured her.

"Do you ever think about being free?"

Soozie's dark lashes veiled her eyes. She looked away from Victorine's glance. "Most folks think about freedom, sometime," she murmured.

Victorine looked down at the carefully prepared food, the fine bone china and fresh linen cloth, and found her appetite gone. Everything about their way of life had changed. The storm was upon them, and old sureties were rapidly fading.

As soon as Soozie left, Victorine put aside the tray, rose, and fetched her hat and gloves. With Colette's note tucked into her reticule, she was prepared to carry out her plan. When Soozie returned for the tray and looked at her in surprise, Victorine shook her head. "I don't need you, Soozie."

Her maid looked shocked. "But, mamzelle, you can't walk on the streets alone. What your papa say?"

"He's at the bank. He won't know if no one tells him!" Victorine's tone was firm.

The maid looked close to tears. "Please, mamzelle. Maybe I be whipped if he hears you been out by your own self."

"When have you ever been whipped?" Victorine was revolted by the thought. "I wouldn't permit it. Just stay out of sight," she continued, scarcely recognizing herself as she

126

spoke. "You can mend the lace on my second-best petticoat. I'll be back well before dinner, and Papa won't know I've been out alone."

She hurried out the door before Soozie could argue further, walked rapidly down the street, then paused to study Colette's scribbled directions. Pulling down the veil on her bonnet to shield her face, Victorine set out.

Near the Ramparts she found the street of small, neat houses, although by now her feet ached from all the walking. At the end of the lane a carriage awaited its owner, the driver yawning as the horses stamped their feet, tails swishing.

Screening herself behind the carriage, Victorine peered at the small, blue-painted frame house halfway down the block. Posies grew in windowboxes, and lace curtains hung at the window. It was not at all the sordid love nest she had expected. Could Colette be mistaken?

But even as she wondered, Victorine recognized the horse tied to the post in front of the house. That was André's favorite bay, with the white streak down its nose. Victorine's stomach knotted in pain. Was it all true, then?

As if in answer, the front door opened and André came out. Laughing, he paused to speak to the slender young woman who smiled up at him.

She was beautiful, with long dark hair pulled up into a knot at the back of her head, a few loose curls escaping around her face. Her nose was tiny and pert, her brown eyes bright with intelligence. She wore a day gown of sprigged muslin, neatly cut and respectable.

Victorine's spirits plummeted. This was the brazen hussy?

But watching André bend to give his *amoureuse* a good-bye kiss stiffened her wavering resolve. Victorine gritted her teeth and ducked behind the carriage as he mounted his horse. She would have died of embarrassment if he had glimpsed her there. But he rode away whistling, as if he had not a care in the world, as if Yankees were not soon to be in control of the city, as if he had no commitments to another woman.

When he was out of sight, Victorine took a deep breath, then marched to the cottage and knocked quickly, before her courage failed. In a few moments the door opened again, and Victorine stood face-to-face with the dark-haired beauty.

The young woman looked puzzled. "Yes?"

"I need to speak to you," Victorine declared.

"Do I know you?"

"I am André Valmont's fiancée," Victorine said, her jaw stiff and her shoulders braced.

Instead of cringing, the other woman raised her chin, her expression calm. "Come in."

Keeping her back straight, Victorine was shown into a minute parlor, with furniture less elaborate than she was accustomed to but still perfectly presentable. The wallpaper showed roses climbing a trellis, and the mantel was of carved oak.

The other woman motioned for her to sit, but Victorine remained standing. She met her rival's eyes firmly.

"I want you to stop seeing Monsieur Valmont."

The woman blinked, her expression guarded. "And why should I do that?"

Victorine forgot her nervousness in a rush of anger. "Because he will be my husband, and I his wife. Because you have no right to his love, no right to disrupt our life together! This is shameful!"

"Shameful?" Now the other woman raised her voice, too. "You call it shameful to love one man with all my heart, as he loves me? I will love him until they put me in my casket, and God willing, beyond. He *is* my husband in the eyes of God, if not under the law. And he loved me before he ever met you!"

Victorine felt her hands clenching unbidden

into fists. She found she was breathing hard. "He doesn't love you. He proposed to me. You were only an amusement!"

The woman's dark eyes flashed. "An amusement? You, who were chosen by his parents because your breeding is above reproach, who will be mated like a cow by a farmer, you talk to me of love? I laugh at you. You will leave my house!"

"How dare you talk to me so!" Victorine felt tears of rage blur her vision. "You are a slave!"

"No, I am a free woman. André saw to it."

"But you are a person of color. Your mother, your grandmother—" Victorine faltered, not sure how far back to go.

"Yes, my grandmama's mama was from Africa. I am not ashamed to say so. André says when he was a student in Paris, the French paid little attention to such things. It opened his eyes to the foolishness of our customs. He would like to be my husband!"

"His parents would never permit it," Victorine threw back, then saw the other woman hesitate, her eyes clouding. Before Victorine could follow up her advantage, a sound from the floor above made her pause.

A baby wailed.

The other woman turned, her expression concerned. There was no doubt in Victorine's mind that this young woman was the mother. And the father?

She felt physically ill. A child, there was a child. How could this woman be just a passing fancy?

"I must leave," she muttered, keeping her head high as she stalked to the door. But when she stood in front of the house, Victorine trembled so hard that she had to lean against the post to keep from collapsing into the dusty street.

André had a child with this woman of color. And this woman knew that his parents and Victorine's papa had arranged the match. Had André discussed Victorine with his mistress, told her of the plans made for his future?

Victorine felt her face burning with embarrassment. She would not believe it. It could not be so. How much of this tale had been spun by a woman desperate to keep her lover, her protector, the man who paid her bills? Was all of it or any of it true?

She marched home, forgetting her fatigue and sore feet in the greater pain of her aching heart. She had barely touched the knocker when Soozie tugged open the heavy door. Despite her earlier protestations, Victorine felt a flicker of alarm. "Is my papa home?"

Soozie shook her head, her relief obvious.

"No, mamzelle." She took Victorine's hat and gloves; then Victorine climbed the stairs slowly to her room. She sat down at the small rosewood desk that had been her mother's and wrote a note to André, asking him to come as soon as he could. She could not wait any longer to have her questions answered.

She sent off the note with a footman, then waited in a fever of impatience. Pacing up and down in her room, she paused only long enough to glance into the looking glass, to tuck up a straying brown curl. Her cheeks were flushed and her eyes bright; under different circumstances, she would have been pleased at her appearance.

André was announced just after four o'clock. Victorine nodded when the butler brought the news. Trying to appear calm, she walked slowly down the stairway to the small parlor, where she found André waiting. He bowed with his usual grace, bending low to kiss her hand.

"My dear, you look well. I trust you've not let the commotion in the city distress you? It is only a passing inconvenience. I do not think the Yankees will have the nerve to hinder us too greatly."

Victorine stared at him. "I want to know if you love me."

It was not what she had planned to say, and

for a moment she felt almost as startled as he looked.

"*Comment?* My dryad, how can you ask? Have I not sued for your hand in marriage?"

"Do you love me? I need to know." She felt strangely calm as she met his eyes; he looked away from her steady gaze. Had he always evaded the word? Why had she not paid more attention?

"You will bear my name and preserve my honor, receiving all the attention and protection due my wife." André's smile had faded. "What is this about? Are you well?"

"I'm quite well, thank you. Is there another woman whom you care for?"

His eyes flashed, and she saw a small vein in his temple throb. "*Mon Dieu*, this is not seemly! This is no question for a lady to ask."

"*Comment?* Why not?" She had a curious sensation, as if the small room had opened up, as if the distance between them had grown much larger. He seemed suddenly far away.

"If your *maman* were alive, she would explain it. Ladies do not speak of women of the world; it does you no credit." His tone was pompous and aloof.

"So there is another woman. I will not have it, André." Victorine lifted her chin as he frowned. Until mere days ago, she had never argued with a man. Now she had defied her father and was placing demands upon her fiancé. No wonder that André looked angry and shocked; she hardly knew herself.

"What are you saying?"

"I'm saying I will not marry you if you have an arrangement with another woman. I want a husband who loves me, who spends his time at home with me, not with a lover."

He flushed and turned away from her. "You have no right to tell me how to run my life! This is no concern of yours."

"I do n-not agree." Her voice wavered once; then she took a deep breath and controlled it again. "If you are to be my husband, it is very much my concern. I will not be a wife who turns her eyes away from your other household, your other woman."

"Someone has been telling you tales!" He turned back to her so suddenly that she stepped backward. "I demand to know who it is. I shall challenge him to a duel to the death!"

She shook her head. "It's not a tale. I have seen her, André."

This time he was the one who looked stunned. "You have met Bella?"

Bella; that was her name, then. Victorine nodded. "And I have seen you together."

He did not protest. He raised one hand, covering his face. When he spoke again, his voice was softer. "It was only a brief fling, my dryad. All the young men have their springtime *amours*. It meant nothing; it is over."

When I saw you this very day? Victorine wanted to shout at him. *When I heard the cry of a baby, your child?*

But André's eyes were filled with pain. It was too much for her; she could hold on to her resolve no longer. She loved him, she did, and surely he must love her back, love Victorine, not Bella in the blue cottage.

When André took her hand again, she did not pull away but allowed him to press his lips to her palm. Shivering a little over the sensuous touch, she tried to believe what he had told her.

They talked a little; she poured him a glass of wine, and then he left for a dinner engagement.

But as she watched his retreating back, the terrible doubts returned. With André by her side, holding her hand, she could forget her worries, believe that his words were true. But as soon as he departed, the question returned to haunt her thoughts, even her dreams.

Whom did André love?

Chapter 9

"The crowd pulled down the Federal flag from the Mint?" Victorine exclaimed. "How brave!"

"But also foolhardy," her father said gravely. "They tore it to shreds. Now Farragut has threatened to bomb the city if Federal flags are not respected."

The thought of New Orleans under attack made Victorine catch her breath.

"If the levee were broken by shelling, the whole city would be flooded," her father continued, his voice tired. "Farragut told the mayor he could have forty-eight hours to evacuate women and children, but that is an impossible task for a city of over one hundred and forty thousand residents. I fear for your safety, my child. If you had not been so disobedient, you would be far away by now."

Feeling a wave of guilt, Victorine knelt by her father's chair. "Papa, I prefer to stay with you. There is no safe place. This war rips apart every Confederate state."

Monsieur LaGrande shook his head. "At any rate, you must stay off the streets. The city's mood is still very volatile."

This time Victorine nodded meekly, genuinely frightened by the sullen anger of the people. She had stood on the lacy iron balcony off her bedroom and watched the crowds thronging the streets, their faces filled with resentment and rage.

"But I have better news, *ma petite*," her papa added. "The marriage contract has been completed; you may begin planning the *déjeuner de fiançailles*. We will set the wedding for the first Monday in June, God willing."

Victorine nodded again and didn't point out that she could not have conducted all these festivities if she had gone upriver. The engagement breakfast was an important custom, though it would be hard to organize properly with the food shortages.

I will not allow this war to bring my own life to a standstill, Victorine told herself. *I must carry on!* Yet she could not order her wedding gown from Paris, as she had always planned; instead, it must be made by a local seamstress.

But while she planned menus and made up

lists of relatives and friends to invite, and the butler ushered in dressmakers laden with fabric swatches and books of patterns, New Orleans's last hope flickered and died.

"The forts have fallen? Oh, Papa!" Victorine exclaimed when her father, grim-faced, broke the news.

"There was a rebellion in the ranks—the same men inside the forts who have been fighting so bravely turned against their own commanders. They had heard New Orleans was taken; then there was a rumor that the officers might blow up the forts, men and all."

"We would never destroy our own men," Victorine protested.

"Worse yet, my French business friends say the fall of New Orleans may discourage Britain and France from recognizing the sovereignty of the Confederacy. It is a grave blow."

Victorine shut her eyes to hold back tears. Her father patted her shoulder. "We will not give up," she said fiercely. "Our Confederate forces will fight back and drive the Northern rascals to their knees! I will not despair."

And with so much to do for the hastily arranged engagement breakfast, Victorine had little time to grieve for the city's fall.

The breakfast was lightly attended. Tante

Marie was far away on an upriver plantation, Colette was in Baton Rouge, and many other people had fled the city. Still, the remaining friends and relatives turned out bravely. Even with fewer guests, Victorine and André had little time to talk, and no time alone.

Only when he presented her with the engagement ring did Victorine feel a thrill of delight. She stared at the large ruby surrounded by sparkling diamonds set in yellow gold.

"A symbol of my undying devotion," André told her.

Victorine smiled as her papa beamed at them both, and an elderly cousin peered nearsightedly past her elbow to examine the ring more closely.

"Thank you, André," Victorine said softly.

"A toast to the happy couple," André's father called, and the household slaves hurried to refill the glasses.

By the time the last cousin and uncle and neighbor had departed, Victorine wanted only to take her throbbing head upstairs and lie down. Their party had been a success, but as hard as Victorine tried, she could not forget the events taking place around them. She said good-bye to André and received a chaste kiss under the approving eyes of his *maman* and *papa*, then left the slaves to clean up the remains of the meal.

In her bedroom, she picked up a letter from Rosamund, which she had received early that morning but had had no time to read. Tearing open the travel-stained missive, she eagerly read Rosamund's rounded script.

Dear Victorine,

Sad news; you have probably heard by now of the bloody battle at Shiloh, Tennessee. Southern forces came so close to victory, but were forced back by Grant's army. General Johnston died, as did over ten thousand Rebel soldiers, and many Union men as well. So many good men dead, so many mothers and wives and sisters weeping! We have already heard of three boys from our county who died on the field. We were frantic over Daniel's safety, but at last had word that he was wounded in the thigh but is recovering. Uncle Tyrone says many Confederate forts on the Mississippi will fall because of this defeat.

We have had our own war losses; Yankee soldiers stole our best milk cow.

I hope you are well and your marriage plans proceeding. I often think of you, about to marry, and Elizabeth, still pining over her missing Yankee sweetheart. I'm the only one of us not yet to have fallen in love—it makes me feel even more lonely. Sometimes I wish we were back again in the schoolroom—what good times we had! Take care, my dear friend.

Love,
Rosamund

Sighing, Victorine sat down at her desk and pulled out a sheet of writing paper. Dipping her pen into the ink, she wrote,

Dearest Rosamund,

I am so happy your brother was not badly hurt.

I was indeed shocked to hear of the battle at Shiloh; we heard first it was a Southern victory, but then sadder news arrived. We could spare little thought to the defeat as we have had our own battles to fight and—it grieves me to write—to lose. It is true what you may have heard —New Orleans has fallen to Federal forces, a navy fleet under David Farragut. He slipped past the forts and made his way to the city, demanding its surrender. General Lovell had no means to fight a battle afloat, with the Union ships overlooking the city, so he had to withdraw.

But the citizens are very angry; no one here would take down our Confederate flag. The Union officers had to do it themselves, and the mob around City Hall was so angry, 'tis a miracle the officers were not killed on the spot. On May 1, General Butler landed his troops, and they marched through the streets while their band played "Yankee Doodle."

Only later, past midnight, did I hear a faint tune drifting through the empty streets—the soft strain of "Dixie." I wept for our city and for the blow to our Confederate cause.

But amid the gloom over the city's fall, I have had happy times, too. The wedding contract is concluded, and we held the engagement breakfast today. It lasted most of the day, as Creoles do love a party, but at last everyone has returned home. The ring André gave me is lovely, a fine ruby set inside a circle of diamonds. The wedding date is set for the first week in June; I only wish you and Elizabeth could be here to share my joy. I pray An-

dré and I will be happy together. I'm sure
we will, except . . .

Victorine paused, then scratched out the last
word and signed her name quickly. Even to her
old friend, she did not want to admit that she
still doubted André's love.

General Benjamin Butler wasted no time in
asserting his rule over the conquered city.
Victorine read in the now heavily censored local
newspapers of the martial rule Butler had declared over New Orleans and the pledge of alliance to the Union that all citizens would be
required to sign.

"Renounce my alliance to the Confederacy?
Never," Victorine promised herself. She tossed
the hapless paper across the settee. "I will never
sign it!"

Yet a few days later, her father came in looking even more worn than usual. "I had to sign
the pledge, *ma petite*," he told her quietly, signal-
ing for the butler to pour a glass of wine. "Otherwise they would have closed down my bank."

"Oh, Papa." Victorine hugged her father, trying to comfort him. "It's not your fault; I understand." His sagging shoulders made her ache.

How dare the Yankees wound his pride in this way. It was intolerable!

Victorine's mood was shared by many. She was too ladylike to spit on the Yankee soldiers, as poorer women and street urchins often did, but she did sew black bows to the sleeves of her best dresses, to show her mourning for their city's fall. And when she walked through the streets with her maid, she pulled her veil over her face and averted her eyes from the men in blue who marched through the streets as if they owned the pavement.

Then, on May 16, came another blow. Reversing his earlier decision, General Butler announced that banks could no longer deal in Confederate banknotes; they must return to U.S. treasury notes or banknotes and gold and silver.

"But the bank has no gold left. I exchanged almost all for Confederate specie," Monsieur LaGrande explained wearily to his daughter.

Victorine was shocked by his gray face. She had never seen her father look so old and defeated.

"He is, indeed, a beast, as they call him in the street, this Butler," she declared fiercely. "I hate him!"

She spent a sleepless night, worrying about her father, wondering what would become of them if the LaGrande bank failed. Would they be out on the street or become pensioners dependent on the charity of relatives? It was unthinkable.

How could her wedding to André proceed if she had no dowry to take to him? How could they even pay for the elaborate wedding feast or the silk dress the seamstresses labored over? Victorine tossed and turned all night.

The next day she rose early to go to market, hoping to escape her anxious thoughts. With Soozie behind her, carrying a large basket, Victorine stepped carefully through the mud and filth that littered the streets. Eyes down beneath her veil, skirts lifted slightly as she tried to keep her hem clean, she did not see the soldier until a pair of blue trousers and muddy shoes came into her circle of vision.

Startled, she looked up.

A young Union soldier, his blue uniform still almost new, grinned impudently at her.

"I think you're the prettiest Secesh miss I've seen so far. Why don't you lift that veil and give a smile to a poor soldier?"

He had red hair and freckles sprinkled across his nose. His blue eyes were friendly but his smile too familiar. Victorine was proud to be a Southern secessionist and in no mood to smile at one of their conquerors. Disgusted, she lifted her chin and stepped back too quickly, losing her footing. She heard Soozie gasp, but the maid could not reach her in time.

The soldier grabbed her arm.

Victorine went rigid with shock. How dare this man, a stranger and an enemy, touch her?

"You are no gentleman, sir!" she protested, straining against his grip. "Let go of me this instant."

His smile turned to a frown. "Hey, I was only trying to help. Your temper's as bad as the aim of your Southern marksmen, missy." He released her abruptly. Victorine, still off-balance, fell backward, landing with a plop in the muddy, manure-spotted street. She put her hand down to steady herself, inadvertently getting a handful of the sticky, smelly goop. Her stomach churned at the noxious smells.

Victorine's anger overflowed. These invaders had taken her city, were ruining her father's bank; now they would accost her on the street? It was too much.

"Our *ladies* have better aim than your cowardly gunmen, sir. It's easy enough to fire on a helpless city!" Without stopping to think, she flung the handful of mud at him.

"We never—" he began, then cursed as the

dirt splattered his clean uniform. "You little vixen! You'll pay for this."

His face red, he hauled her to her feet. He pulled her light veil away from her face and stared at her rudely, as if to fix her features in his memory.

Victorine forced herself to stand still in his grip, trying to look haughty and unafraid, though her heart pounded so hard that she thought her whole frame must be shaking.

He grabbed her arm, dragging her along the crowded street.

"Let go of me!" she demanded. "What are you doing?"

"Taking you off to the calaboose," he told her. "Ain't you read the new General Order? Women who insult our forces can be thrown into jail."

Victorine felt weak. Into the Parish Prison, with ordinary criminals? Her vision darkened, and she heard loud ringing in her ears.

He braced her as she swayed. Her limp weight was an awkward burden for the young private. Soozie ran along beside them, then took off in another direction—no doubt for help.

The soldier paused, and his anger seemed to fade. "Hey," he said, relaxing his hold. "If you apologize nicely, maybe—"

Victorine swallowed hard, willing the darkness away. It was her chance. She could say she was sorry, and he might let her go.

But she wasn't sorry, not in the least. "Never!" she exclaimed, straightening her petite frame with great effort.

The private blinked in surprise. Victorine jerked back, turned on her heel, and ran.

"Stop!" he yelled.

She heard him pounding through the mud behind her; she tried to run faster, but her corset cut into her ribs, and she couldn't get a deep breath. This was hopeless. Any second he would lay hold of her again, and she would be thrown into jail.

Behind her there was a collision, followed by muffled exclamations and the shrill chatter of fowls. Victorine glanced back as the Yankee soldier let out a string of curse words.

A cart of chickens for the market had come between her and her pursuer. The stout woman pushing the cart winked at Victorine, then turned to the soldier. He was barely visible behind the frantic chickens squawking and beating their wings. Feathers flew into the air.

"So sorry, dearie, I didn't see you," the woman said loudly.

"This way!" another woman in a ragged

cloak hissed at Victorine from the shadows. Victorine ducked into the alley and ran on, gasping for breath. It seemed forever, but within minutes she stood at her own home, shaking with fear and weariness as she pounded on the door.

She ignored the shock on the butler's face as he stared at her filthy dress and the hair cascading about her face.

Victorine pushed past him. Behind her the door closed, and she shivered with relief. Would the soldier find her?

"Oh, mamzelle, you be safe," Soozie called, clapping her hands. "I sent for your papa; he on his way!"

The maidservant helped her upstairs. In her room, Soozie quickly pulled off Victorine's ruined frock and brought hot water for her to wash with.

"Burn that dress," Victorine said, her teeth still chattering. "I never want to see it again. And not a word of this to anyone else, you hear?"

"Yes, mamzelle," Soozie agreed. "Those Yankees, they come and take you to jail, no?"

"Not while I have any fight left in me," Victorine said.

She was tucked into bed when Monsieur LaGrande hurried home.

"*Ma petite*, you are safe? *Mon Dieu*, what is

next?" He looked worried. "Did you not hear about the new General Order authorizing soldiers to throw women in jail? You must leave the city at once. The wedding will have to be postponed."

"No!" Victorine shook her head stubbornly. Not for any reason would she delay her wedding. With André by her side day and night, she would fear neither the red-haired soldier nor the rest of the wicked Yankees.

*C*hapter 10

The next morning Soozie burst into Victorine's room, an empty basket on her arm. "Oh, mamzelle!"

"What is it?" Victorine looked up from fastening the long row of buttons on her dress. "Did you see that Yankee soldier at the market? Did he threaten you?"

"No, mamzelle." Soozie shook her head, tears trembling on her dark lashes. "It's M'sieur André, mamzelle."

"What? Tell me, quickly!" A dozen awful thoughts flashed across her mind: *André has volunteered for the army and been shot; André has been taken ill; André*—

"He's fighting a duel, mamzelle. Madame Valmont's maid, she told me at the fish shop. She seen him slip out of the house early, and heard him speak to his valet. He's there this minute, fighting for the honor of 'the woman he loves,' she says. Oh, mamzelle, what if he get himself killed? Then you have no wedding!" The maid sobbed aloud.

Victorine stood frozen, unable to answer. She felt as if time had stopped. She would stand here forever, trapped by her own fear, while the man she loved died in a duel for her honor. This was the result of her stupidity in publicly assailing the Northern soldier. Had someone jested unwisely about her brawl—who was the other man? But it didn't matter. André fought to protect her good name. *Oh, dear God*, she thought. *Pardonnez-moi! I have killed him!*

Ignoring Soozie's sobs, Victorine grabbed her shawl and ran down the stairs. She had heard of these duels—foolish, she'd always thought them. Her papa had tried to explain how important a man's honor was; she knew hotheaded young men sometimes fought and died over trifling matters. She also knew, from listening to her papa and his friends sharing stories, that there were two likely meeting places for duelists: the dueling oaks or behind St. Louis Cathedral in St. Anthony's garden.

The cathedral was closer. She would pray that they were meeting there, pray she was not too late, and that André would not die because of her foolish temper.

For the second time in two days, Victorine

hurried through the streets, breathless from the sharp pain in her side while her corset pinched her fiercely. But she ignored the discomfort, would not slow down because of her ragged breathing or her heart, which beat loudly.

When she saw the sharp spires of the cathedral, she paused to catch her breath, then slipped around back, past the tall evergreens that made this spot secluded and private.

Yes, they were here. Past the trees she could see men talking together, and she recognized André's handsome profile, his impeccably tailored suit. Another man offered a carved rosewood box. She watched in horror as André pulled out a slim, wicked-looking dueling pistol. The man crossed the grassy space and offered the box to the other man, who did the same. She didn't recognize the other duelist, but again, she knew duels could spring up over the most casual remarks. And her rash action at the market yesterday could have sparked jokes around the city.

It was a disgrace for her to be here. The duel itself was nothing unusual, but her presence would cause a scandal the whole city would hear of. And she knew André was an excellent shot. He might emerge unscathed.

But she could not take the chance. And even if he was the victor, he might have to leave town if his opponent died. Either way, she would lose the man she loved, only weeks before their wedding. She must stop this madness.

She heard the rustle of feet shifting on pine needles and looked up. Shocked, she saw a man standing only a few feet away.

"Mademoiselle?"

It was Dr. Whitman! Victorine stared at him, trying to marshal her thoughts. The doctor was neatly dressed in a dark suit; he was taller than most Creole men, with broad shoulders and dark blond hair.

He examined her closely. In her haste, she had come out without hat or veil or gloves. She pulled her shawl over her head, trying to shield her face, but it was too late. Then she remembered the urgency of her mission; nothing else mattered.

"I must stop the duel," she whispered, nodding toward the men gathered on the grass.

"I fear that will be impossible; I tried my best to reason with them, but they are both young and hot-blooded," he told her. "It's a waste. If they wish to kill themselves, they should at least do it in the service of their state."

She almost nodded in agreement, then realized how disloyal that would be. "But it is for

154

honor," she murmured. She might question André's actions, but for someone else to criticize—

"What kind of honor requires a man to throw away his life?" the doctor answered. "Life is too precious."

"If you think this is so foolish, why are you here?" she asked tartly, offended for André's sake.

"Because doctors are scarce, he is your fiancé, and I do not wish you to be unhappy," he said, this time not meeting her eyes. "And, I admit, I need a pass to get out of town to rejoin my regiment. Valmont has better connections than I, and more money for bribes."

She suddenly realized that a Confederate officer should not be in the city at all. Her eyes widened.

He nodded again. "I know. I should have left when the city fell, but my mother was dying."

She heard a tremor in his tone and for the first time noted the mourning bands on his coat sleeve. "I'm sorry," she murmured. "I, too, lost my *maman*, years ago." Without thinking, she touched his hand gently.

He gripped it for a moment, his fingers warm against her bare skin. Belatedly aware of her unladylike behavior, she knew she should pull her hand away. But his grip was so firm, so comforting; unfamiliar feelings stirred.

Then she blinked and stepped back. The duel! How could she forget, even for a moment? André was still in danger.

"I must stop them," she protested. "André is fighting over me. It would be my fault if he were killed!"

The man in the center had backed away. She saw André turn, his pistol uplifted, and the two opponents took measured steps away from each other. One of the other men counted aloud.

Victorine lifted her skirts. If she had to dash between them and risk taking a bullet herself, so be it. It would be a major scandal, as well, but to save André from death—

"Mademoiselle, they fight over a woman named Bella," the doctor said quietly.

Victorine thought her knees might give way. "What?" *Bella—Bella is the woman André loves?* Victorine loved André as she had never loved anyone, and he was fighting over someone else? She thought her heart had broken in two—the pain was overwhelming. Victorine couldn't breathe; she hurt all over, and her vision blurred. Far away she heard shots ring out, then a muffled shout.

She forced her attention back to the scene in front of her. "Is André hurt?"

"No, it's the other poor devil," Dr. Whitman said grimly, picking up his bag. "I must go. Better you stay out of sight."

Victorine felt relief for André's sake, but it was far off. Her pain was too great. It wiped out everything, her hopes for her marriage, for a happy life with André by her side.

Bella was the woman he loved. It was all true, then. All the doubts Victorine had fought so hard to vanquish returned in a rush, all the shadows took on new substance. Bella had told the truth that day at the little blue cottage. Despite everything André had said, he loved Bella, and he had proposed to Victorine only to appease his parents and to produce an heir approved by the laws of their state.

Victorine looked down at the gold ring on her finger, the large ruby glowing as sunlight glinted off its encircling diamonds. It felt suddenly heavy. Her old nurse used to say that the ring finger carried a vein that went straight to the heart. If so, both were numb now. Past the pain, Victorine felt a deepening coldness inside her. The love she had prayed for, André's love, was not for her.

She could no longer bear the weight of the

ring. She pulled it off, almost cast it aside into the shadows under the trees, but instead she held it tightly inside one fist.

The men had gathered around as the doctor tended the wounded duelist. Victorine stepped farther back into the trees so that no one would glimpse her. She knew she should leave now, but she had one more thing to do.

With mounting impatience she watched as several men lifted the wounded man and carried him away, while André turned to speak to someone in his party. Finally Dr. Whitman walked slowly back to her hiding place, his jacket slung over his shoulder, his sleeves rolled up, a trace of blood still on his hands.

Victorine shivered at the sight. "Is he—"

"No, he'll live, this time," the doctor told her. He looked at her searchingly. "You're very pale. Are you all right, mademoiselle?"

Victorine felt tears close to the surface. She swallowed hard. "I think I, too, will be leaving the city soon. But would you do me one favor, *s'il vous plaît?*"

He nodded. "Let me see you home."

She shook her head quickly. "Just give Monsieur Valmont this. He will know what it means."

She held out the ring, and the doctor took it, his brows lifting. He looked back at her, his eyes suddenly alight. "Only if you allow me to see you safely to your family."

She stared up at him, feeling tears she could no longer control sliding down her face. She couldn't answer.

"I will not tell them where you have been," he promised, his tone low. "I will not come inside and anger your father again. I only want to protect you. The streets are not safe. Please?"

Victorine nodded, throwing her shawl over her head and tugging it forward to hide most of her face. She didn't watch as he walked back to give André the ring; she slipped past the trees to be completely out of sight. The doctor rejoined her a few minutes later. They walked back to the LaGrande town house, and he bowed over her hand before she slipped inside.

"If you need me again, send word to this address." Dr. Whitman handed her a card. "I will leave town soon, but I would do anything I can to assist you."

Victorine could not confess her double shame to her papa. Ladies did not attend duels. It was easier to allow him to think she had listened to his counsel at last and agreed to leave the city. A pass was arranged and her trunks quickly packed. But Victorine would not go to Tante Marie.

Victorine could not bear to hear her aunt exclaim over the virtues of André and the Valmont family, nor was Victorine ready to explain the disaster that had ended her engagement. Colette she could talk to; Colette would understand. She would go only to Baton Rouge, the state capital, not to her uncle's plantation deep in bayou country. Reluctantly, in the face of her growing agitation, her father agreed.

Over the next two days, André sent her several notes, but she refused to answer, refused even to read them. Her only venture outside the house was a visit to the cemetery where her *maman* and little sister were interred. Heavily veiled, Victorine left Soozie waiting at the cemetery gate and walked slowly to the elaborate vault that belonged to the LaGrande family.

She had been coming here for years. Those new to the city were often startled to see all the tombs above ground, but New Orleans lay too low and was too swampy to bury the dead otherwise. She opened the vault's iron door with a rusty key and walked inside.

The air was still and musty, but not unpleasant. Withered roses lay on her *maman*'s casket. Victorine brushed them aside and divided a fresh bouquet between her mother and sister. Then she knelt and counted her rosary beads as she said prayers for their souls, now at peace with the angels.

"I miss you, Maman," she whispered when the last prayer had been said. "If you were here, you could tell me what to do. Papa would not understand; he would think all this is nothing. But my heart is broken. I cannot bear that André loves another. I do not think you would counsel me to marry a man whose heart belongs to someone else, no matter how good his family, how wealthy his estate. Help me to know what to do, dear Maman."

She laid her head against the cool marble slab and allowed her tears to fall unchecked. She was so alone, and her heart ached as if the wound were a physical one. She almost expected to see a visible rent in her flesh, but the gray dress she wore was untouched. Her chest rose and fell rapidly as she sobbed, but the hurt was in her soul.

At last Victorine stood and pulled the veil down to hide her face. She walked home slowly, with Soozie a few paces behind her.

Chapter 11

At dawn the next morning an ancient carriage pulled up in front of the house. Several pieces of luggage were already lashed to the top. Victorine would be traveling to Baton Rouge with two other women who were taking shelter outside the city.

"This Confederate officer—he will join you on the outskirts of town?" Victorine's father asked.

"Yes, Papa," Victorine replied, not quite meeting his eyes. When he had learned of Victorine's plans, Dr. Whitman had offered to escort her to Baton Rouge, and Victorine had readily accepted. She knew his protection might be needed, and his presence would bring her comfort.

Luckily the war had distracted Monsieur LaGrande. He seemed to assume that the officer was an acquaintance of one of the other women, and did not press Victorine for details.

"Good, you will have an escort." Monsieur LaGrande gave his daughter a final embrace. "Hurry, the carriage is at the door, and the other ladies are already inside."

Victorine dabbed at her eyes as she left the house, fixing her gaze on the waiting carriage. She was leaving New Orleans and didn't know when she'd return. Joseph had stowed her luggage; he helped her aboard. Then, with a crack of the driver's whip, the carriage was off.

Dr. Whitman met the women outside town and rode beside the carriage as it bounced and jolted northwest to Baton Rouge. The journey would have been easier by water, but by now Federal ships controlled most of the river.

Throughout the journey Victorine thought of André's handsome face and his faithless heart, and she wept silently. Wiping her face often with a sodden handkerchief, she pulled her veil down to hide her swollen eyes and reddened nose.

"Poor child," the gray-haired lady next to her said. "Have you lost someone in your family?"

Victorine lifted her handkerchief again. "Forgive me, I can't bear to talk about it."

"Oh, I know so well," the woman sighed. "When my nephew died . . ."

Victorine let the conversation flow past her, still lost in her own pain. She had no wish to tell the whole story, to admit her humiliation. She hadn't even told her father; he thought the marriage was only delayed, the ring put away for safekeeping.

When they neared the town at last, the carriage stopped on the outskirts, and they climbed out stiffly to stretch.

Dr. Whitman spoke to Victorine in a low tone. "I must leave you here; the Yankees have already been this far, and I don't know if any linger in the town. I have to go farther to find my company."

"Are Yankees nearby? Will there be a battle?" Victorine asked, wide-eyed at the thought of more conflict.

"I don't know. But I've heard guerrilla fighters in the region may provoke the Union men. I hope for your sake there is no disturbance here and your stay will bring the sparkle back to your eyes. Perhaps someday you will consider another man's courtship?" His blue eyes were hopeful.

Victorine looked down, suddenly shy. "I don't know; I can't think of that right now," she murmured. "God keep you safe."

He bowed over her hand, his grip firm and reassuring. To her own surprise, she felt a pang at the thought of his absence. She was the last of the women to climb back into the carriage, and

Dr. Whitman waited to see them approach the town before he turned his horse toward the trees. Peering out from behind the leather curtains that protected them from dust, Victorine felt even more alone as he disappeared from sight.

Her heart lightened when the carriage rolled up in front of the white frame house that belonged to Colette's family. A shriek from inside the house told her that she had been seen, and a slave came to help her down. While she hurried toward the house, he unstrapped her heavy trunk from the carriage.

Colette rushed down the walkway. "Oh, Victorine, I am so glad to see you!"

Victorine felt her eyes flooding with tears. She blinked them away as she returned her friend's hug. "And I you, *mon amie.*"

"What is it? You look so sad. Was the journey difficult?" Colette took her arm as they walked slowly toward the house, where Colette's large family gathered to greet Victorine.

"I have much to tell you," Victorine murmured. "Later."

"Oh, *ma petite.*" Madame Dubois, her plump form swathed in layers of shawls, embraced her. "We are so glad to see you. Is New Orleans quite devastated? Is Beast Butler as much of a brute as we have heard? Tell us all."

With Colette's younger brothers and sisters flocking around, Victorine was taken inside.

She told them her tales of New Orleans, all except those pertaining to André, and Madame Dubois was volatile about the hated invaders. "How dreadful for you, my child! I am glad you have come to us."

In turn, they told Victorine how the Union naval commander, David Farragut, had proceeded up the river after taking New Orleans. He had paused at Baton Rouge but continued to attack Vicksburg, Mississippi. The state legislature had hurriedly moved inland weeks earlier. Now the fear was that the Federals would return to Baton Rouge.

"My neighbors say we should retreat into the woods, but what are we to do, sleep beneath the pine trees like animals? Live on pinecones and swamp grass?" Madame Dubois, who despite her ample frame was always in frail health, shuddered. "*Mon Dieu*, may the angels look out for us!"

They ate a simple but substantial evening meal, and finally Victorine could retire to the bedroom that Colette shared with two younger sisters. When the young girls were asleep in the trundle bed, Victorine sat on the big bed, whispering her story to her friend.

"And when I learned that the duel was over the octoroon woman, what else could I do? Papa doesn't know that I've ended the engagement—I told him I put away the ring for fear of theft, with so many soldiers about—but I cannot marry André now." Victorine sobbed.

Colette patted her shoulder. "Maman says a wife should ignore these things, but my sister is so miserable. I don't blame you, *mon amie*. He is not worth a lifetime of loneliness. Your home should be a comfort, your marriage full of all those things most worthy—love and respect and honor."

Victorine smiled through her tears. "I knew you would understand."

They talked for hours; then, for the first time since she had given André back his engagement ring, Victorine slept soundly, worn out by her travels and her heartache.

For the next ten days she joined Colette and her family in a simple household routine that soothed her wounded spirits. In the morning they all gathered in the sunny dining room for breakfast. Then, leaving the clearing away to the household slaves, she and Colette shepherded the children upstairs and supervised their lessons. Madame Dubois spent most of her time lying on her chaise, a little sewing the most rigorous activity her health would allow.

Victorine had to swallow a giggle when she thought what Elizabeth and Rosamund would say if they could see her playing tutor; she had never been the most devoted scholar at the Academy. But now she helped little Marie Annette and Margaretta with their arithmetic, and Benjamin and Simon with their counting; then she and Colette stood over the children as they traced their letters and heard them read aloud, haltingly, in both French and English.

After the midday meal, the young ones were tucked in for a nap and Victorine and Colette could lounge on the bed with a yellow-backed novel. Later they would tend the flower beds while the children played nearby, or stroll around the block. If it rained, they did needlework, mending clothes.

In the evening after dinner the family often gathered in the parlor and sang together as Colette strummed her guitar.

"We'll have 'Dixie' first," Colette suggested. She led them in a rousing chorus of "Away, away, away down south in Dixie!"

" 'The Bonnie Blue Flag' next," Victorine begged, and sang as loudly as she could. "Perhaps Beast Butler will hear an echo of it to disturb his sleep," she whispered to Colette, and they laughed, in spite of their mutual worry over New Orleans's future.

If Madame Dubois's head ached too much for music making, Victorine and Colette would take turns reading aloud to each other while they plied their needles. But this made it too easy for Victorine's thoughts to wander. Although the visit here had eased her unhappiness, her heart still felt cold and empty.

Sometimes, if memories of André pained her too much, she thought instead of Dr. Whitman, with his kind blue eyes and husky voice. She thought of the way he had held her hand so tightly, and it made her stomach prickle. She confessed to her friend that she would like to see him again.

"But *mon amie,* he is not Creole!" Colette said.

"I know." Victorine sighed. Besides, no one would ever take André's place, no one would have his dark good looks or polished manners. No one would send her heart pounding as André had or give her so much happiness when he smiled into her eyes.

But André was lost to her. Blinking hard, Victorine pricked her finger with her needle and had an excuse to wipe her eyes.

*   *   *

The morning of May 28 began much like the rest. Victorine and Colette had just shooed the children upstairs and settled them around the big table they used for lessons. Victorine leafed through the pages of a French grammar book.

"Margaretta, don't pull your sister's hair," Colette commanded, taking her seat at the head of the table.

A sudden commotion made Victorine look out into the hall.

Downstairs their housemaid ran into the house, dropping a basket of potatoes. The basket overturned and the vegetables rolled across the smooth wooden floor.

"A guerrilla fighter done shot a Federal officer on the ship, and they going to shell the town!"

Victorine felt a wave of fear so intense she thought she couldn't breathe. *Don't the Yankees know that most of the men in town left with the army? They'd shell women and children and helpless old people?*

A sudden boom shook the house. Victorine grabbed the doorframe for support. She dropped the book, her heart beating fast as the children screamed.

"It's cannon fire!" Colette cried. "We'll all be killed!"

Victorine shut her eyes for a moment. Everything came back: how the Charleston schoolhouse had shaken when the cannons roared their assault on Fort Sumter. But then, though the houses had rattled and smoke had filled the air, the town itself had not been the target. This time they were under attack. She felt sick with fear. She wanted to run to her bed and pull the covers over her head.

Then she looked down and saw the children, all sobbing aloud. Margaretta, who was six, had tears streaking her face, and her eyes were wide with terror.

Victorine bit her lip. She knelt quickly and put her arms around the little girl's trembling body. Margaretta clung to her, throwing her arms around her neck.

"Hush," Victorine warned her friend, nodding toward the sobbing children. "We must stay calm."

"Colette, little ones," her mother called from below. "Come quickly, we must get out of town, *tout de suite!*"

Cannons roared again, and Victorine heard a crash nearby as angry metal shattered wood.

"Come," she told Margaretta, lifting the little

girl in one arm and giving her other hand to Marie Annette, who was nine.

Colette took the little boys, and they hurried down the steps.

Madame Dubois threw her shawl around the smallest boy. "Hurry," she called. Their house-maid, Annie, came running with two freshly baked loaves of bread in her apron, her expression alarmed. The other slave had already run out the back.

More cannon fire shook the house, and the children shrieked. Margaretta sobbed again and put her hands over her ears. Victorine wanted to cover her ears, too, but her hands were full with the children. She pushed through the outside door behind Colette and joined the frenzied crowd in the street.

Smoke drifted from the river, and the streets were filled with citizens, mostly women and children, some barely dressed, all running for their lives.

Every time the cannons boomed, screams rose from adults and children alike. Pushing her way through the crowd, Victorine panted from the weight of the little girl in her arms and tried to hold on to the other child. *This must be what hell is like*, she thought, *confusion and fear and no protection anywhere*.

Cannon fire thundered again, and Madame Dubois stumbled and fell. Dropping her loaves into the dusty street, Annie struggled to pull her mistress up. Colette put down her little brothers and knelt in the dirt to help her mother. Victorine paused, too, trying to catch her breath.

"I cannot make it; you must go on without me," the matron said, holding her side. Her face was pale, except for bright spots of red on her cheeks. "Save the children."

"No, Maman, I will not leave you!" Colette looked frantic. She helped her mother up. With Annie on one side of Madame Dubois and Colette on the other, the boys beside them, they stumbled on. Victorine came behind with the little girls.

She thought perhaps none of them would live to tell about this day. Once Victorine heard a strange whistling noise. Looking up, she saw a dark, evil-looking shell flying a few feet over their heads. It exploded into a house just beyond the street. *Madness*, Victorine thought. *Don't they see it's only women they're shelling?* But she had no breath to speak, except to urge on the children, the maid, and Colette and her ailing mother.

They reached the edge of town and stopped a

moment under a tall tree to rest. The road was still full of fleeing families.

Victorine tried to swallow. Her mouth was so dry, it felt as if it were carved out of rock. The sun was high now, and it beat down on her uncovered head. She felt flushed and hot and completely parched. She had no hat, no veil, no gloves, nothing except the dress she wore, which was already dusty and dirty from their hasty retreat.

What would become of them?

Chapter 12

They spent the night huddled in the woods, trying to comfort the hungry children. Victorine felt dirty and damp, and her empty stomach ached. She thought longingly of the bread that Annie had dropped in the street; Victorine would willingly have rubbed away the dirt and chewed on the plain loaves. Her throat ached for water. When she felt clammy dew on her bare hands, she sucked the light drops, trying to ease her thirst.

Never before had she been exposed to so many dangers. Victorine watched Annie, her admiration growing. The Dubois house slave made no complaint, spending the long night humming to the little boys. *Perhaps, as a slave and a black woman, Annie is much more accustomed than I am to facing hardship,* Victorine thought. Then a child whimpered for her attention.

Victorine could have sobbed herself, but she hid her own despair as she rocked little Margaretta in her arms, trying to lull the child into closing her eyes. It was difficult to sleep; they were all too uncomfortable and hungry.

When dawn came, stragglers still wandering out of town reported that the shelling had ceased and all appeared quiet.

"But the Yankees are threatening to confiscate abandoned homes," a woman told them, "and rebel guerrillas say those who return are traitors and will be tarred and feathered!"

Victorine glanced at Colette. "What shall we do?"

Colette shook her head. "My mother can barely walk, and the children will all have fevers from the damp night air. At least back in town we have shelter. We cannot lose our home. We shall have to go back."

Victorine stood up, her back aching; she winced from painful new blisters on her feet. With the ailing Madame Dubois and the children, they made slow progress. When the sun rose higher into the sky, it beat down on their unprotected heads, and Victorine felt dizzy from fatigue and heat and thirst.

Margaretta jerked away from her hand. "Water!"

Past the road, Victorine saw water, green and

sour-smelling. "No, no." She grabbed the child back. "It will make you ill."

Yet she, too, had to fight the impulse to rush to the stagnant water and drink from its murky depths. Swallowing hard, her throat dry and scratchy, she urged Margaretta on.

Stopping often to rest, they entered the outskirts of town in late afternoon. As they passed the first few buildings, Victorine saw a wooden cistern. Water!

Leaving the rest of her party, she ran across the yard, sending hens fluttering and squawking, and shoved aside the heavy wooden cover. An empty crock sat on a nearby bench; she used the crock to lift out clean rainwater and drank eagerly.

Nothing had ever tasted so good. The freshness eased the pain in her throat; she could feel it all the way down. She gulped it so quickly that rivulets ran down her chin and spotted her dirty gown, but Victorine, usually so neat, didn't care.

A cry from the road reminded her of the rest of her group. Ashamed to think that for a moment she had forgotten them, Victorine dipped out more water and took it to her friends.

They passed the heavy container around, helping Madame and the children drink. Victorine refilled it twice before she put the crock back on the bench and covered the cistern. Then, with new energy, they walked the rest of the way home.

The Dubois house showed no damage, although across the street a neighbor's porch sagged dangerously where a Union shell had sheared away two pillars before caving in the side of the house.

When Colette opened the front door, Victorine saw potatoes still littering the floor. She stopped to pick up as many as she could grasp, tumbling them back into the basket. Her stomach rolled at the sight of food.

"Get your mother into bed, and I'll help Annie prepare something to eat," she told her friend.

Nodding, Colette supported her mother in her slow ascent up the stairs, with the children following behind.

At Annie's direction, Victorine mixed cornmeal into a thin gruel while Annie peeled potatoes and fried bacon. They boiled the potatoes and made tea, then called the rest of the family.

Colette took a bowl of gruel to her mother while Victorine dished up the simple fare to the children, who ate eagerly.

"Not too fast," Victorine told them. "Your

stomach will send it all back." But she, too, found it hard not to wolf down the first food she had tasted in a day and a half.

Afterward they heated water and helped the children bathe. Then Colette assisted her mother with her toilette, and Victorine was able to lather herself with rose-scented soap.

Later, pulling on a soft, clean cotton gown, Victorine thought how rare and sweet were the small luxuries of life. To eat a meal and drink fresh water, to bathe and feel clean clothing against your skin, to sleep on a bed with a pillow beneath your head and a roof above to keep off the damp—these were great riches. She felt her blessings tonight as she never had in her luxurious New Orleans home, with her silk gowns and French perfumes.

At school Rosamund and Elizabeth had gently teased Victorine about being pampered; now Victorine knew they'd been right. *How things have changed*, Victorine thought with a sigh. Reflecting on the lessons of war, she drifted into sleep.

The next day she wrote to her papa, telling him they had survived the shelling. Then she and Colette took a basket and went to replenish the larder. Although his shelves were full, the storekeeper refused Colette's Confederate banknotes.

"But this is all we have," Colette told him.

The man nodded toward the Union officer examining a keg of salt a few feet beyond. "Orders," he said.

Victorine glared at the startled officer. "We have children to feed," she snapped. "You'll starve the babes as well as blast them away? I did not think even Yankees were such cowards!" Her face flushed with anger, she picked up her basket and hurried out of the store, leaving their groceries sitting on the counter.

Colette caught up with her on the street. "Oh, Victorine, you must learn to mind your tongue. That soldier asked the storekeeper who you were and where you lived!"

Victorine stared at her friend, guilt overcoming her anger. "Surely they would not blame you or the children for my rashness! If they take me away to prison, well, so be it. It will not be the first time I've been so threatened."

They trudged home, baskets swinging empty on their arms. Away from town, their Confederate money might buy them a little to eat, but they had no place to shelter, and supplies in the countryside were already low. Here in Union-controlled Baton Rouge, they had no currency with which to purchase food.

"The garden will soon be producing," Colette murmured. "If we can make it that long with the little in the pantry."

Victorine nodded, trying to hold back tears. War was not the glorious adventure she had once thought, all brave songs and new uniforms. This was the reality of war, trying to feed the children, praying your home would not be reduced to rubble.

Back at the Dubois home, no one had the heart to hear the children's lessons. They gave them a holiday and allowed them to play on the floor with wooden blocks and a hand-carved set of Noah's ark, which soon had Margaretta and Simon quarreling over who would guide the elephants up the ramp.

Victorine took a novel and went to sit on the long front porch. She was the first to see the wagon pulling up to the gate, with a blue-coated soldier holding the reins.

Her stomach seemed to turn inside out. Would she be arrested? General Williams had already taken away some townsmen.

"Colette," she called in a weak voice.

Coming to the doorway, her friend gasped. Victorine put aside her book and sat up very straight. She was a LaGrande, a Confederate patriot, and she would act as bravely as she could, even though she was only a woman.

The officer who opened the gate and walked up to the front steps looked familiar; she recognized him from the shop.

"Mademoiselle Dubois?"

"My friend is Mademoiselle Dubois," Victorine corrected, surprised at how steady her voice sounded. "I am Mademoiselle LaGrande. You have something to say to me?"

Instead of answering, the officer motioned to his men. To Victorine's astonishment, she saw two men wrestle with a heavy barrel, then roll it through the gate and up to the porch.

"Where would you like it put, ma'am?" the officer asked politely. He had faded blue eyes and a mustache just beginning to gray. He looked at her kindly, she thought with surprise. Had he left a family somewhere up North?

"What is it?" Colette called from the door.

"Flour, ma'am. I understand you have need of it."

Victorine blinked and glanced back at Colette. How could they take food from their enemy? She saw Margaretta and little Simon peeping from behind their sister's skirts, and she knew the answer.

"Thank you, sir," she told the officer steadily, swallowing her pride with less effort than the old haughty Victorine would have expected. "You could take it around to the kitchen, if you would."

Bowing, he directed the men. They left the flour, then lifted their hats and drove the wagon back up the street.

Across the way, Victorine saw one of their neighbors, who had been watching from her own porch, shake her head.

"We may be branded traitors, accepting aid from the enemy," Colette murmured when she returned from seeing the precious flour safely stored.

"At least the little ones will eat," Victorine said grimly. "What else could we do?"

"He was very polite. I thought all Yankees were like Beast Butler," Colette said. "War is full of surprises."

Victorine nodded. "I could wish for some healthy tedium."

Colette giggled, and in a moment Victorine laughed, too. They went to see about dinner, thankful for a replenished larder.

The next afternoon Annie came to find Victorine, who was mending one of the children's aprons. "A man brought you a note, mamzelle."

"Who?"

"He gone now," the slave said. "But he said you could leave an answer under the woodpile, and someone fetch it."

Victorine ripped open the note, which was written in an unfamiliar hand.

Dear Miss LaGrande,

I hope you and your friends are safe after the shelling. It was a monstrous act. You must feel you have gone from the frying pan into the fire.

I hope you do not regret your passage north. At least I had the pleasure of your company. When I lie down to sleep at night, I remember how your dark eyes shine and your right cheek dimples when you smile. I hope you are soon smiling again. God bless you and keep you safe.

Respectfully,
Brent Whitman

Victorine felt a pleasurable warmth as she reread the note slowly. He had not forgotten her, busy as he must be with his men. He had worried about her. The short message had none of the flowery grace of André's love letters, yet it lifted her heart. Victorine smiled to herself, then blushed when she saw Annie watching her with curiosity.

"You going to answer the young man?"

"What makes you think it's a gentleman?" Victorine asked, her tone dignified. "Never you mind."

But Annie grinned as she left. Victorine hurried up to the schoolroom to find paper and pen, hoping her answer would make its way back to the Confederate doctor. How far away was he? She couldn't ask, and he would not be able to answer. But he was thinking of her. She smiled again as she climbed the stairs.

The days resumed their leisurely rounds, and Victorine hoped that the worst was behind them. But there was always the chance of another attack. Colette and her mother debated, then decided to do what many local families had already done.

One dark night when the moon was behind a cloud, Colette and Victorine crept quietly out into the back garden, carrying a shovel and several heavy bundles wrapped carefully in strong linen. They dug holes beneath the rosebushes and buried the family silver, then replanted the bushes to hide the evidence of their digging.

Victorine felt the ache in her back as she bent to her task. She smelled the musty rich scent of damp earth and heard crickets crying in the mellow darkness.

"I've made another blister," Colette whispered. "But if we have to leave again, or the Yankees blow up our house, at least something will be saved."

That was not the only digging they did; they had new chores to do. Willie, the Dubois slave who had tilled the garden and a field of corn at the outskirts of town, as well as doing heavy household chores, had disappeared.

"Do you suppose he was killed in the attack?" Colette worried. "Or has he run away?"

They had no way to know, but in the meantime, the precious vegetables had to be tended. While Victorine's blistered feet healed slowly, she raised new calluses on her hands helping hoe and weed in the large garden, while faithful Annie toiled in the cornfield. Madame Dubois had only enough energy to watch the children, and even they sometimes labored with their big sister over the rows of carrots, potatoes, and beans.

"You must wish you'd stayed in New Orleans," Colette said one warm afternoon as they worked in the garden together.

Straightening slowly, Victorine pushed a strand of damp brown hair back under her bonnet. Her shoulders ached, and her cotton dress was limp with perspiration—she had never worked so hard before. But she shook her head.

"If I were still in New Orleans, I might be in prison," she said grimly. "There is no safe place to be, not in this war."

For a moment, she remembered sitting in the opera beside André, his handsome smile quickening her pulse. How long ago that seemed. She thought of parties and fine dresses and the joy of planning her life, with a wedding to stage, a household to set up, married life and babies to follow.

Now what did she have? Blistered palms, sore muscles, and a sunburned nose. Would she ever have cause to smile again?

Abruptly, Brent Whitman's face appeared in her mind's eye. His blue eyes were so kind, his smile understanding. She wished she knew where he was, if he was still safe. Sighing, she bent back to her weeding.

A week later Victorine received a letter from her father. He was well, and so were the servants. The Yankees were firmly in control of New Orleans, and General Butler continued to arrest and imprison citizens, both male and female, who openly professed Confederate sympathies.

Her father also enclosed a sealed letter from André, which Victorine tore into pieces without reading. Somehow, the blow of his betrayal was fading. She felt pain, but not overwhelming anguish, as she tossed the shreds of paper away.

Her father made little mention of business, but from his comments, she suspected that the LaGrande bank was still struggling. If this war stretched on, who knew what the end would be? Would they be penniless?

Even the course of the war itself was a mystery. With the Yankees in control of the newspapers, it was hard to get reliable news of the conflict beyond their state, but they heard rumors of Confederate victories in Virginia and Tennessee that renewed Victorine's hopes for the South.

"Come quick, Victorine," Colette called on a muggy morning in late July. "It's General Williams's Federal troops, back from Mississippi and their attack on Vicksburg."

"A sad-looking lot," Victorine said as they watched the ambulances and wagons full of sick soldiers roll through town.

As a loyal secessionist, Victorine knew she should feel cheered by the weary troops who marched behind the wagons. Yet she felt a pang of sympathy, too. Their faces were gaunt, their bodies thin, their shoulders sagging. Some looked hardly strong enough to carry their guns.

"Did our forces do so much damage?" she wondered aloud.

"More likely Williams's men were felled by dysentery and malaria," Colette answered. "The Yankees aren't used to our hot, damp climate."

The wan, sickly men in the ambulances rumbling by seemed to confirm her guess. Even the horses and mules looked bedraggled.

"There's the general himself," Colette whispered. Victorine stared. General Williams sat erect and proud on his horse, his whiskers and beard neatly trimmed, his uniform spotless. What a contrast to the troops he led! She wondered how much sympathy this stiff bandbox soldier had for his ailing men. They had heard rumors that he drilled his troops tirelessly, even in the summer heat.

A few nights later, Victorine heard a male voice at the back door. Madame Dubois and the children were already in bed. She and Colette had been reading in the parlor; they were alone on the first floor, except for Annie.

Alarmed, Victorine picked up the iron poker from the hearth and hissed to Colette, motioning toward the back of the house.

"What is it?" Colette dropped her book.

"I don't know; it sounds like a man."

Colette's face was pale. "Do you think I should call Maman?"

"Don't alarm her yet," Victorine murmured. Gripping the poker tightly, she tiptoed toward the back. Colette picked up a candle and followed. Outside, in the pale glow of moonlight, Annie spoke to a shadowy figure.

"Who's there?" Colette called.

Annie shrieked in surprise, and the man turned toward the soft light from the house.

"It's only Willie, mamzelle," the missing slave answered.

Colette lifted the candle as the slave stepped into the faint light. Victorine saw that the man's face was gray with fatigue and his clothes were torn.

"What's happened to you? Where have you been?" Colette demanded.

"The Yankees, they was digging a canal at Vicksburg, to move the river so they could take the town," Willie explained, his voice tired. "Hundreds of slaves worked a long time—some fetched off plantations by the Yankees, some runaways—to be free, mamzelle."

Victorine swallowed hard. She had once thought that well-treated slaves didn't mind their condition. She was learning that she had been wrong.

"So why are you back?" Colette asked.

He hung his head. "When they didn't take the town, the Yanks just left us, mamzelle. General Williams, he promised we be freed, but he left us. I don't have nowhere to go. I ain't ate in three days. If rebel guerrillas find me—they hang runaways, mamzelle. You let me come back?"

Colette sighed and lowered the candle. "Annie, fix him something to eat. And Willie, next time, you be more careful whose words you believe."

With Willie back, there was less hard labor for the women to do. Victorine spent more time indoors, hoping that the new and unfashionable tan on her face would soon fade, the calluses on her hand heal.

Perhaps there was hope for an uneventful August, and the constant rumors of a new attack would prove false. But on the morning of August 5, she woke to the blast of gunfire.

Chapter 13

Jumping out of bed, Victorine ran to the window. Thick fog shrouded the town; she could hardly see the neighboring houses. Gunfire rang out again.

In the trundle bed, Margaretta shrieked in alarm. Victorine hugged the child. "Don't be afraid, Margaretta. Let's get dressed now, just in case."

Colette also rose, her expression anxious, and they quickly got the little girls into their clothes. Then Victorine pulled on her own dress and hastily pinned up her hair. She took out the small carpetbag she had readied for another flight. It held her hairbrush, pins, powder, toothbrush, all the small necessities; a nightgown and one dress, extra stockings and underthings, an extra pair of shoes, the miniature portrait of her mother, a small volume of French poetry her father had given her. The bag was stuffed full, but at least she was prepared if they must run again.

"Come down, *tout de suite!*" Madame Dubois called. "Hurry!"

Victorine heard the heavier roar of cannons now, and the whistle of a shell all too close to the house.

They stumbled down the stairs and found Madame Dubois pacing the floor, her widow's cap slightly askew. "A neighbor stopped to tell me that our Confederate troops are attacking. But the armies are fighting hand to hand in the streets, and the Yankees are shelling the town again. We must get the children away."

Victorine clutched her bag; Colette had another with the children's clothes and some of her own. Annie, looking frightened but bearing up bravely, helped Madame Dubois and carried a soft travel bag under the other arm.

Had Willie disappeared again? Victorine had no time to ask.

Outside, the fog was lifting, but patches of haze still obscured the view. Victorine could hear shouts and the rattle of gunfire, and heavy cannons boomed in the background. They hurried down the street, stopping in alarm at a crossroads when they saw armed troops struggling a few blocks ahead. Shots rang out; then a man in tattered brown jumped a picket fence. He let loose with a hoarse rebel yell that seemed to echo endlessly: "Wa-who-ee!"

Victorine was caught between excitement—these were their men, fighting back at last—and fear. Bullets were flying too close, and the children's faces were white with terror. She took Margaretta's hand, and she urged her to hold on to her sister. They all turned and ran down the lane, trying to skirt the skirmishes taking place all around them. Layers of acrid smoke drifted through the hazy air. They coughed as they ran.

The streets were filled with people, some half dressed, many crying aloud with fright, shouting and cursing, carrying strange collections of items they had snatched up as they fled. Victorine saw an elderly lady puffing as she lugged a large mantel clock in her arms; a young woman clutched her baby and what looked to be the remnants of a wedding veil.

Victorine felt a terrible sense of *déjà vu*. She had lived this before. It was all happening again, the fighting, the running, the fear. What would become of them?

The streets were now even more crowded with people; many of the roads out of town were blocked by the fighting.

"We'll have to go south, down River Road," Colette called. Victorine followed her friend's lead, with Madame Dubois and Annie behind, all struggling to hold on to the children as they pushed their way through the panicked crowd.

When they reached the edge of town, they paused to drink from a cistern near an empty house, then walked on more slowly. The crowd of fleeing residents was less dense here.

A black man passed them in a rough farm cart, and Colette called to him. "Sam, is that you?"

He pulled up the old mare and peered down at them, fanning himself with his straw hat. "Mercy, Miz Colette? Madame Dubois, you here with all the children?"

"Yes, Sam. Where are Madame Halsey and her family?"

"They gone to the plantation, ma'am. I got to get the horse and some food out before the Yankees stole'm. You need a ride?"

"Do we? Oh, my!" Colette looked at her struggling family.

Victorine said, "Put your mother and the children up."

It took both of them and Annie to push Madame Dubois over the side of the cart. The children were next. Adding five passengers atop the bundles and boxes filled the small vehicle to overflowing, with Annie perched on the narrow seat beside Sam.

"But I cannot leave you, girls," Madame Dubois fretted, clutching her youngest son as she perched atop a barrel of meal.

"We'll go much faster on our own," Colette assured her mother. "Just knowing you are all safe will be the biggest help. We'll meet you at the Halsey plantation; I'm sure they'll take us in if they can. Get along, Sam, and bless you. You're an angel in disguise."

The old slave clucked to the mare, and the overloaded cart rolled down the road.

Victorine smiled wanly at her friend. Now it was just the two of them. She picked up her bag, and they trudged on. Her carpetbag grew heavier by the hour as the sun overhead burned more brightly. *I must endure*, Victorine told herself, wiping her damp forehead. Another long and dusty march, and they would find friends to take them in till they could return home. This day would not be such a disaster, after all.

But just as the monotony of the walk had lulled Victorine into thinking they were safe, gunfire rang out sharply over their heads. Victorine glimpsed men in the trees firing and saw puffs of smoke emerging from the barrels of long guns.

"Look out!" she screamed. Colette ran into the trees. Victorine followed, into the tall pines and swampy ground.

In her panic, she felt a buzzing past her cheek and couldn't tell if it was bullets flying or insects roused by her wild flight. She dared not stop to find out.

She ran until her corset threatened to suffocate her; the tightly laced garment would not allow her to draw a deep breath, and running made her head spin. Where was Colette? Victorine staggered one more step, her vision blurred. The tall trees spun dizzyingly around, and the ground rushed up to meet her.

She came to with rough grass prickling her cheek and the smell of earth in her nostrils. Scrambling unsteadily to her feet, Victorine tried to think. Where was she? Had she lost Colette? Panic threatened again, but she pushed it away.

"Colette?" she called, hoping her friend was safe and nearby. But only the drone of insects answered her, and a flutter of wings as birds in the treetops above flew farther away.

She was alone. She must return to the road and find the Halsey plantation where Colette would be seeking her family. Wearily Victorine brushed leaves off her skirt, picked up her bag, and set out again.

All the trees looked alike, and she no longer knew which direction to take. She could not find the road, or any path, and as the light faded, her fears grew.

Then a crackle of brush made her freeze. "Who's there?" a youthful voice called out.

"It's only a civilian," Victorine answered, her voice wavering despite her best efforts. "I'm lost and unarmed."

She heard more tramping as he came closer; then she saw a soldier hardly old enough to shave, his uniform ragged. But it was a brown uniform, and Victorine drew a deep breath. Not Yankees, then. Perhaps it was even Confederate regulars, more disciplined and dependable than the guerrillas.

"Captain, over here," the private called. "I done found a lady."

When she saw the man who came in answer, Victorine cried out in surprise. "Dr. Whitman!"

Brent Whitman hurried forward, grasping her hands. "Mademoiselle, are you hurt? What are you doing here?"

"The attack on the town—we had to get away from the fighting—I lost my friends." The words tumbled out, and tears sprang into her eyes. She was so relieved to see him; his blue eyes were as kind as always, and his grip warm and welcoming.

"Take the lady's bag, soldier, and tell the rest of the men to continue their search for wounded," Dr. Whitman ordered, almost absently. "I'll escort the lady back to camp."

"Yes, sir," the soldier said cheerfully. He picked up the carpetbag, then walked off to rejoin his comrades.

Looking up at the tall American, Victorine tried to regain her dignity. "Thank you. You've come to my aid yet again. I hope you do not find it a tedious habit."

"I could never find you tedious," the doctor said simply. He plucked a dead leaf from her tangled hair, then smoothed its unruly curls, his touch gentle. "I'm overjoyed to find you safe. Can you walk back to camp?"

"Of course." But when she tried to straighten, her knees buckled. The doctor moved swiftly, and Victorine found herself lifted easily in his arms.

He cradled her against him, his arms reassuringly firm. Victorine shut her eyes for a moment, feeling his heart beating beneath the wool uniform, which scratched her cheek, his chest rising and falling with each breath.

She had never felt so at home, yet this was

scandalous—she hardly knew him. She should demand to be put down at once. Instead she opened her eyes and smiled up at him. He bent his head, then hesitated.

"I would not take advantage of your plight," he murmured. "It's miracle enough that you should be here."

Victorine touched his cheek gently. "You would not," she agreed, her smile heartfelt. She slipped her hand behind his head, and in response, he lowered his lips to meet her own.

Their kiss began gently; then his arms tightened, and his kiss became more urgent. Victorine felt her pulse quickening. The feelings that surged through her whole body surprised and exhilarated her—this was nothing like André's polite and practiced embrace. She returned the kiss with eagerness and joy.

Brent Whitman raised his head at last. "I think I should get you back to camp," he said, his voice husky, "before I forget that you are a lady, and I a gentleman."

Victorine smiled. She had absolute trust in her new suitor, but she couldn't suppress a glimmer of mischief in her smile. "If you forget, I'll remind you," she murmured. "But you could kiss me again before we go."

And he did.

A bird calling in the treetops ended the long embrace, and Brent shook his head. "We must get you to shelter. You need food and rest."

Victorine nodded, resting her head against the scratchy cloth of his uniform. His rapid pace across the uneven ground lulled her eyes shut as the fatigue of a long and difficult day caught up with her. He carried her with apparent ease, while she drifted in and out of sleep until she was put down on a pallet inside a small tent. Then she slept again, too weary even to say good-night before the doctor was gone. But knowing he was nearby took away all her fears, and she felt secure once more.

When morning came she woke to find that someone had placed her carpetbag beside her and covered her with a blanket. Stretching, she thought briefly of her rescue and the brief interlude in the forest. Blushing a little, she smiled at the memory. But the sound of someone moaning close by forced her thoughts back to the battle, and to Colette. What had happened to her friend? Was she safe?

Victorine pushed herself up. When the wave of giddiness passed, she stood, a little shaky at first, but gaining confidence when her legs supported her. She lifted the flap of the tent and stepped out.

She was in an army camp. She saw tattered gray and nut-brown uniforms, a few mangy tents surrounding a campfire, and many more wounded from the recent battle overflowing the shelters. Nearby, without even a blanket to cushion them, she saw men lying on the damp earth, restless with pain and shock.

Victorine felt a wave of shame. She had slept inside a tent while dying men lay in the mud. It was not right. "*Mon Dieu*, give me courage," she murmured, kneeling to wipe the bloody forehead of a private burning with fever. A young orderly came out of another tent, his expression twisted.

"Who's in charge?" Victorine called out. "Where's Dr. Whitman?"

But the orderly bent almost double with pain, folding his arms across his stomach as cramps racked his body. "Can't wait, ma'am, this dysentery . . ." He ran behind the tents toward a crude latrine amid the trees.

Victorine walked toward a large tent. Inside, a man screamed and then went silent. Victorine shivered. Would the doctor need her help? Could she, dare she, try to face the bloody wounds and shattered bodies that a battle left behind?

Her schoolfriend Elizabeth had aided the wounded soldiers after the Battle of Manassas, near Bull Run in Virginia. But Elizabeth had always been brave, whereas Victorine shuddered at the mention of blood. When Madame Corday had instructed the older girls at the Academy about medical aid, after the conflict had begun, Victorine had hung back, protesting, even though the teacher had told her she had a nimble hand with bandages.

Now her stomach rolled at the thought of facing men wounded in battle. She turned aside, blinking hard against tears. It wasn't fair; this was expecting too much. She would return to her tent and stay out of the way. Surely that was the most that could be expected of her. But another man groaned. She hesitated, then walked slowly to the large tent's entrance.

Victorine paused in the opening of tattered canvas. A lantern hung from the tent pole, and boxes were stacked along the sides. In the middle, a patient lay sprawled on a crude platform of wooden planks held up by sawhorses. Dr. Whitman, his shirtsleeves rolled up, bent over him.

"I need help here," the doctor called. "Hurry, man."

But there was no one to help, no one except Victorine. She felt her stomach twisting as she saw the blood splattered everywhere and smelled the odors of illness and death. Yet even as she put up one hand to cover her nose, she stared at Brent Whitman.

He looked around, and she was shocked at the fatigue that dulled his eyes and made his shoulders sag. Had he slept at all last night? He blinked at her in recognition, smiling briefly.

"Mademoiselle, you're awake. I'm glad. Have you seen my orderly? I'm desperately in need of some assistance, lest this man bleed to death under my hands."

"The orderly—I think he's ill." She took one step back and swallowed hard, feeling the bile rising in her throat as she saw the blood that darkened the doctor's arms.

The doctor frowned, wiping his forehead and leaving a streak of blood across his brow. "I see. Are you able—"

He paused, and Victorine shuddered.

"No, I think not. If you see my aide, please urge him to hurry back." There was no reproach, but Victorine heard weariness in his voice as he leaned back over the patient.

She stepped backward, eager to flee the carnage and foul odors. But something held her. These men were fighting for the cause she believed in; if they gave their lives, their health, could Victorine not bear a little discomfort? How hard was it to control a cowardly stomach?

"Tell me what I can do," she said quietly.

Dr. Whitman looked at her with approval. He gestured at a bar of soap and a bucket of water. "First, wash your hands thoroughly."

She quickly complied. Then he said, "Put your hands here, below the patient's wound, and try to slow the bleeding so that I can find the shell fragment. If I cannot close this soon, I'll have to amputate the leg, and his chances of surviving will be small."

Victorine pushed where the doctor pointed, just above the raw angry wound. She tried not to breathe, gritted her teeth to control her queasy stomach when blood splashed her hands. She would not be ill, she would not swoon; a man's life hung in the balance.

Dr. Whitman probed with the scalpel, then grunted to himself. "There! Can you hand me the forceps? Yes, the long ones."

Still pressing against the man's skin with one hand to lessen the flow of blood, Victorine reached for the instrument the doctor nodded toward and watched as he carefully pulled out an ugly, jagged piece of shell casing.

"Now, to close this. Then we can only pray he does not succumb to infection," Dr. Whitman murmured. "And there are so many more waiting."

Victorine kept her position and watched as he finished the surgery. Then she helped bandage the wound, packing it with dry lint to absorb any seepage. The young aide returned in time to help Dr. Whitman move the injured man to a pallet on the ground, and they lifted another soldier, bloodstained and limp, onto the wooden platform. Then, looking greener than Victorine felt, the young aide slipped away again.

Dr. Whitman looked at her. "Do you wish to go back to your tent? I know this is not a pleasant scene for a lady."

To her own surprise, Victorine shook her head firmly. "As long as I can help, I will stay."

He smiled, and Victorine felt a surge of pride. She had not run away. Instead she had stood her ground and faced the bloody scene, putting her own fears aside for the sake of the South. Suddenly she felt stronger and wiser and prouder than she could ever remember feeling. She was no longer just a refugee of war, running here and there to escape the bullets. She could be useful. She was needed.

Dr. Whitman's blue eyes crinkled at the corners as he smiled at her. Victorine felt a rush of happiness that she must remember to savor later, because right now the doctor had already bent over the new patient on the rough operating table.

"Forceps," he directed.

Taking a deep breath, Victorine handed him the instrument.

Chapter 14

They worked late into the night, until Dr. Whitman staggered with weariness and Victorine found the lantern-lit tent blurring before her eyes.

"You must rest," he told her. "Go back to your tent."

She shook her head stubbornly. "You should give that tent to the wounded. I am sound of body. They have greater need."

"A lady in the midst of so many men needs privacy," he told her gently. "And if you sleep in the damp night air, you will not be well for long."

"At least give my pallet to some poor fellow," she begged him. "I can sleep on a blanket on the ground. I have had worse since the war began, I promise you."

Brent Whitman gazed at her with obvious admiration. "You are an angel of goodness, mademoiselle."

Victorine felt herself blushing at the extravagant praise. "*Mais non*. It's only simple decency."

She slept that night on a rough woolen blanket, and if the ground beneath the scattered pine
needles was hard, Victorine was too exhausted to
feel it. She slept soundly and woke several hours
after dawn.

She stretched, groaning at the soreness of her
body, and sat up. Still, remembering the mangled
soldiers filling the camp, Victorine felt thankful
that she had two sound legs and two working
arms, stiff though they might be.

A young private brought her a tin cup full of
gruel and a hardtack biscuit, which had to be
dunked into the soupy liquid until the brick-hard
bread softened enough to eat. But she ate it all
hungrily. Then, after hastily pinning up her hair
—she had slept in her clothes—she hurried to
the hospital tent.

There were more wounded to tend to. All
around her, soldiers were still being carried in
from the battlefield, some in worse condition
than the men they had seen yesterday.

She found Dr. Whitman already in the hospital tent. The wooden planks had been freshly
scrubbed and his instruments laid out neatly,
close at hand. He was washing his hands and
arms in a pail of water.

He looked up when he saw her. "Most physicians don't bother," he explained, nodding toward the soap and water. "But one of your sex, Florence Nightingale, showed the world during the Crimean War that more careful hygiene can decrease the number of battlefield deaths. Also, one of the teachers at the New Orleans School of Medicine studied in Paris for a time and heard a man named Louis Pasteur, who thinks illness could be caused by bacteria."

"Back—what?"

"Tiny organisms too small to see." He looked back toward the men lined up in rows outside the tent. "We have more wounded. Several men have been brought in with limbs shattered by cannon fire; some already have gangrene setting in. I must amputate, to give them a chance to live; otherwise, they will die slowly and painfully. It will be even worse than the operations we went through yesterday. I hate to ask, mademoiselle, but you have a steady hand and a kind heart. Can you assist me again?"

Watch a man's leg being hacked off? Worse, take part in this agonizing procedure? It was impossible. Even her newfound strength would not be enough for her to meet this kind of challenge. But Victorine found herself nodding.

"Bless you. I will have the first man brought in."

Dr. Whitman directed his wan-looking aide, and they brought in the first of the wounded. Victorine rolled up her sleeves, tied a length of rough calico around her waist to protect her gown, and washed her hands as the doctor had done. Then, her heart pounding, she took her place at the doctor's side.

The patient on the rough platform was still conscious, though obviously in terrible pain. His blond hair was tousled and dusty, his face so young that Victorine thought of Colette's brothers and bit her lip. His leg was so mangled that Victorine could hardly look at it. The right foot had been shot away completely, and the raw bone of his leg stuck out from the swollen flesh, already oozing pus from infection. The smell made her catch her breath.

"Please, no, Doc, not my leg," the young man pleaded. "I can't go home no cripple. Don't do it, Doc."

"We don't have any choice, man," Dr. Whitman told the private. "If you want to go home at all, this is your only chance. You must hold tight, now."

"But I left a sweetheart back in Georgia;

211

what'll she think, if I come home half a man?" He sobbed aloud.

Victorine felt tears blurring her vision. She blinked hard. "If she loves you, she'll thank God if you come home in any shape," she told him firmly. "Now let the doctor help you."

Dr. Whitman poured chloroform from a glass vial onto cotton and motioned to Victorine to hold it over the soldier's nose. The young man coughed at first, but he inhaled the strong fumes. In a few minutes his eyes closed and his breathing slowed.

The doctor took the private's limp wrist and showed her how to count the patient's pulse. "If it slows too much, give him a whiff of ammonia. But since we are in the outdoor air, more or less, the risk of overdose should be small."

Victorine nodded, too nervous to speak. It was so much to remember, and so much was at stake.

The young orderly, who looked almost as ill at ease as Victorine, slit the wounded man's pants leg up to his hip and applied pressure on the main artery to slow the blood to the leg.

Dr. Whitman reached for his instruments, and Victorine braced herself. There was no going back.

Dr. Whitman cut into the upper leg; even with the supply of blood reduced, a splash of crimson colored his shirt, and his arms were soon red to the elbows.

Victorine fought to breathe, feeling giddy for an instant. She would not swoon, she would not. She had seen terrible wounds yesterday, watched the doctor probe for bullets and shell fragments. She would make it through this somehow. She would not let them down, not the doctor, not the poor boy from Georgia who wanted to go home to his sweetheart.

"We must retract the skin and incise the muscle tissue, but we need to leave a flap to wrap around the bone when we are done." Dr. Whitman spoke as calmly as if he were giving a class to his medical students.

His matter-of-fact tone steadied her. Victorine listened to his voice closely, grateful for his perception. Did he guess how hard this was for her? The tent steadied, and she no longer felt as if the ground were shaking.

"Now I need the saw."

Victorine shuddered as she watched him pick up the surgical saw and apply it to the hard bone of the leg. She had never heard such a dreadful sound as the rasping of the saw against the bone.

The patient groaned faintly, and she held the chloroformed cotton back to his nose.

"Doctor, I can't—" The young orderly suddenly bent over, racked by a spasm of cramping. He lost his hold on the artery, and Victorine saw, to her horror, a sudden new rush of crimson as blood spurted from the wound.

"Hold on, man!" Dr. Whitman snapped. "He'll bleed to death if you don't keep pressure on that artery!"

But the orderly gasped and clutched his stomach. "I can't." Bent almost double, he stumbled out of the tent.

The doctor swore briskly, trying to slow the flow of blood. Victorine stood still for an instant. Then she moved swiftly to replace the orderly, pressing down with both her small hands just where the doctor had earlier directed.

"Yes, yes, that's it," Dr. Whitman said.

She saw the bleeding slowing to a sluggish drip. Visibly relieved, the doctor proceeded to the next step.

"Now I have to tie off the arteries with silk thread," he told her, moving rapidly.

She saw that he had the needles already threaded, lying ready on a clean piece of cotton. She watched his deft motions, thinking of all the embroidery she had done while never dreaming of sewing human flesh.

"Now we use a bone file to smooth the bone, to help it heal," Dr. Whitman told her. "Then we can close the wound."

She watched silently; her arms ached, but she was unable to change her position. Finally the doctor nodded. It seemed as if they had worked forever over the prone man, but by the slight shifting of sunlight outside the tent, Victorine guessed that the surgery had taken barely half an hour.

"You can release your hold."

The patient was stirring. Quickly, before he came to, they bandaged the stump, now clean of the old infection.

"His pain will be great," the doctor said. "But as long as our morphine holds out, I can help." He reached for a small wooden box and drew out a strange-looking instrument.

Victorine stared. "What is it?"

"This is an endermic syringe," Dr. Whitman explained. "They're new, not many doctors have them, but it's a better way to give the morphine. I can inject it right through the skin."

She watched as he filled the syringe with liquid, then stuck the needle into the patient's upper leg. As the young man on the table groaned, Victorine asked softly, "Will he live?"

"Perhaps, if another infection doesn't set in or he doesn't succumb to disease," Dr. Whitman said quietly. "But he has a chance now. Thank God you have a cool head on your shoulders!"

Victorine flushed again. *How astonished Elizabeth and Rosamund would be!* she thought. When she had the chance to write to them, they must hear how frightened little Victorine had grown up at last. Madame Corday would be proud of her, too, and pleased to know that her efforts to teach the girls some nursing skills had not been in vain.

"There are wounded waiting." Dr. Whitman interrupted her thoughts. "Are you up to more surgery?"

"I think so," Victorine told him, smiling.

They worked together all morning, with occasional help from the orderly, then stopped to sip weak tea and eat a hasty meal.

Victorine asked Dr. Whitman about Colette. No one had reported finding another young woman lost in the woods, so Victorine could only hope that Colette had found her way to her friends' plantation. Colette at least knew its direction, Victorine told herself ruefully, whereas she herself had been running blindly through the trees.

Dr. Whitman found a local man who knew the Halsey plantation, and Victorine scribbled a note, asking if Colette had arrived safely, telling of her own situation. She folded it, and the lanky young private grinned at her, then hurried away.

"And the battle?" she asked Dr. Whitman. "Did we win?"

He shook his head. "They fought hard, poor lads. General Breckinridge had marched our men all night; they were exhausted before the fight began. And the general hoped for support from the ram *Arkansas*, which fought so well at Vicksburg; he needed aid against the Union gunboats. But the ram developed engine trouble four miles above Baton Rouge. When Union boats appeared, the crew was forced to set it afire and leave it to burn."

Victorine thought of the Confederate ships in New Orleans, the *Louisiana* and *Mississippi*, which had also been burned to keep them out of enemy hands. Again she wondered why the Confederate naval force had not been better prepared.

"Our men gave as good as they got, and the Yankees suffered losses, too. We've heard that their General Williams was killed during the battle. But when General Breckinridge learned of the *Arkansas*'s destruction, our men had to fall back."

The Northern general was dead? Victorine remembered the stiff martinet of a man who had drilled his blue-coated troops so unceasingly under the hot sun, and she felt little regret.

Dr. Whitman put down his tin cup. "I must get back to the wounded."

Victorine stood up quickly. "I'm coming."

That afternoon they treated a succession of wounded and dying. Victorine became almost inured to the sight of blood and gaping wounds. Almost. She hoped she would not dream of blood and pain when she finally had time to sleep.

At the end of the day, as Victorine washed the bloodstains off her hands, the young private returned with a letter for her.

Colette! Victorine accepted the message with thanks, then hurried to the campfire and scanned the page in the wavering light of the flames.

Dear Victorine,

Thank God you are safe; we were so worried! I made my way to the plantation and found Maman and the children here before me. The Halseys have taken us in, though they are so crowded here with refugees from the town that we are sleeping shoulder to shoulder on the floor, and then the house will barely hold everyone.

Worse news, one of our neighbors stayed through the battle and arrived in the country only this morning.

He says that after our troops were driven back, the Yankee soldiers looted the town, ripping our family portraits, shredding my good dresses, the parlor furniture, stealing anything of value (thank heavens we buried the silver!), pouring molasses over the carpet and wallpaper. I wept to think of our poor house, and Maman is beside herself—to do such a thing to a helpless widow! And then they set it afire. Our dear little house is gone forever. A third of the town at least is destroyed, we're told, and rows of great trees cut down for barricades. I hate the Yankees for taking their revenge on innocent civilians!

But enough, I will tell you the rest later. Come to us; we will share what we have with you, gladly. Your dear friend,

Colette

Victorine wiped her damp eyes. To lose so much so quickly! And to think of men acting like such animals—looting and destroying! What kind of creatures were they? She remembered the courtly Union officer who had brought them flour when they needed food. And now this. Did war bring out both the best and the worst in men?

At least Colette's family also owned a home in New Orleans, where Federal forces were still firmly in control. In that city Yankees had not committed this kind of wanton destruction, though some property had been confiscated by Beast Butler.

Homes destroyed, Confederate currency not accepted . . . would they all be beggared by this war?

"Your friend, is she safe?" Dr. Whitman asked.

Victorine nodded. "She and her mother and the little ones are staying at their friends' plantation."

"I'm glad you have found them," the doctor said, his tone somber. "I'll arrange for an escort to take you there."

Victorine sat in front of the fire, thinking. To be back in a house with other female companions, far away from the blood and gore of the battlefield, was surely tempting. Yet what would Brent do without her? He couldn't tend to all the wounded with so little help.

She glanced at the doctor, and he smiled warmly. Despite all she'd seen, all the horrors of the war, how pleasurable it had been to be near him! "I'm staying here," she said firmly.

He looked at her in surprise. "But, mademoiselle, we will be leaving the area very shortly."

"Then I will go with you." She met his gaze firmly.

"An army is no place for a delicately reared young lady."

Victorine thought of the ravaging Yankee troops and lifted her chin. "With *our* men, I am not afraid. And there will be more battles, more wounded to nurse, yes?"

He nodded. She saw his blue eyes crinkling at the corners as he smiled at her, heard the admiration in his tone. "You're very brave. I pledge to you, mademoiselle, that no one will even think of treating you rudely while I am here."

He took her hand for a moment, pressed her bare fingers in a strong grip. It sparked a thrill of pleasure inside her. This was a man to make any woman's heart beat faster. And there was more.

André would never have respected Victorine's new strength, never have allowed her the dignity of choosing for herself. In Brent Whitman's clear gaze Victorine read respect, admiration, and love. At that moment she could almost feel the last icy corner of her heart flooding with warmth. She knew that André's betrayal would never pain her again.

Chapter 15

"Thank'ee, ma'am," the young private said, his eyes glittering with fever.

Victorine smiled down at him, wiping his hot forehead with a damp cloth. *Sometimes a gentle touch is the best medicine*, she thought. She treated all the wounded men tenderly, as if they had been her brothers. Indeed, she felt they were all one family, fighting together for one cause.

She had sent a message to Colette before they broke camp and enclosed a letter to be sent on to her father. Victorine shuddered to think of his reaction—his sheltered daughter traveling with the Confederate army?

Yet it wasn't completely unheard of. Laundresses and women of easy virtue followed the troops, and occasionally an officer's wife braved the rigors of the field with her husband. Victorine had no fears of the ragged but cheerful soldiers who marched away from Baton Rouge, some tramping the muddy roads without shoes or coats, their courage high.

She sang "Dixie" with them and "Hurrah for the Bonnie Blue Flag" as she bumped along in a baggage cart, and the men cheered.

"Our own Confederate angel," one soldier said as they moved upriver to Port Hudson with General Breckinridge's forces.

In the new camp Victorine worked beside Brent in surgery, changed bandages, and often simply reassured a delirious soldier.

Even when there were no battles, illness kept them busy. She learned to administer doses of quinine for the recurring fevers and to attach black, slippery leeches from the swamp to men who needed to be bled. It made Victorine proud that her nursing skills continued to grow. As she worked daily with Brent Whitman, her respect for his perseverance and courage also grew.

But it was increasingly clear to her that she felt more than respect for this man. When his hand brushed hers, Victorine quivered inside. And when they sat together by a campfire after a hard day's work, if she leaned on his arm, it was not just from fatigue but to relish the pleasure of having him so near. She thought often of the short interlude in the forest, but there was no privacy and no time to repeat it.

One evening they rested, drinking a cup of herb tea, which Dr. Whitman thought good for her health. Boiling the brackish local water with herbs did improve it greatly.

They discussed the day's sick, and then Victorine told him how her mother and little sister had died of yellow fever. "It happened so quickly. I thought her the best *maman* in the world; she was gentle and kind and so beautiful."

"You must be very like her." He smiled at her and took her hand. "Do you think that a Creole could love someone who was not of the same heritage?" His eyes were bright and his grip on her hand almost painful.

Victorine felt her pulse leaping. "This one could," she said, waiting breathlessly for his next statement.

But a wounded man called out from one of the tents. Shaking his head, the doctor rose to answer.

Sighing, Victorine finished her tea. After making sure she wasn't needed, she entered her small tent and lowered the flap so that she could don her nightgown and let down her long hair. But even when she lay on the hard ground, thoughts of the broad-shouldered doctor would not leave her. Did Brent care for her? He must. If only their conversation hadn't been interrupted.

The next afternoon they finished their rounds early. While Brent sat down to write a report, Victorine headed to a nearby creek for water. The apron she had fashioned to protect her dress had been spotted with blood; she needed to soak it and her spare dress to remove the stains.

Filling her pail, she lugged it back up the path. A clatter of hooves made her look up. An elegantly dressed man approached on a dark horse.

"Victorine?"

"André!" Victorine dropped the heavy pail, and the water splashed her skirts. It was like seeing a ghost—their engagement seemed so far in the past. "What are you doing here?"

"Looking for you, of course; your father has been frantic. I've been searching for days. Why on earth are you carrying water like a household slave?" André dismounted; his fine clothes were coated with dust, and his expression was grim.

"I—I—" Victorine couldn't seem to speak coherently; her thoughts flew round like a flock of startled sparrows. "I didn't expect to see you again."

"We are betrothed," André said. "Returning the ring was foolishness. We shall be married as soon as I get you home."

She stood up straighter, anger calming her confusion. "*Mais non.* I'm afraid your trip has been in vain. I'm not going to marry you, André."

His handsome face contorted; she had forgotten how haughty he could look. "Don't be absurd; it is all agreed. Your father—"

"Shall not choose my husband for me." Her heart thudded at her own temerity, but she knew it was true.

"Nonsense, a good Creole girl does not question her father's wishes. My parents have agreed; the contract has been drawn up. And I will honor it, even though your father's bank looks close to failing. I am a gentleman. My word is sacred."

His lofty tone stung. "I am not a charity case, dependent on your honor," Victorine snapped. "And you're the one who is being foolish. How can you wish to marry me when you love someone else? She's borne your child!"

For the first time the mask cracked, and she saw emotion flaring in his dark eyes. "That is not for you to speak of!"

"Why not?" Victorine folded her arms defiantly.

"You should not have knowledge of women who are—who are not of your kind. If you do, through some meddling gossip, a lady would pretend not to know. Our marriage is agreed upon; I must have children who can legally inherit my name and estate. My parents desire it." He spoke stiffly, as if his jaw were tight.

Victorine met his angry gaze firmly. "I am not a brood mare, André. If you wish to keep a wife merely for her breeding ability, you may look elsewhere."

"*Mon Dieu*, this is not ladylike language! What has happened to you since you ran away from the city? Is everyone a savage here, that you have no longer any proper regard for decorum?"

Despite his anger, André was as handsome as ever. But as she stared at him, Victorine saw stark images of the wounded she had cared for, the dying whose eyes she had closed even while she wept. She had learned to deal calmly with blood and suffering, to sleep on hard ground, to prepare her own meals, to put up her own hair. The small rules that had once governed her life seemed to have fallen away like rusty chains.

"André, I have gone hungry, I have been shot at, I have watched men die. Don't speak to me of decorum. It hardly seems important anymore."

"That is why I shall take you back at once!"

"So that I may go to prison?" Victorine asked evenly.

"General Butler is much hated, but rumor says he may be replaced soon," André told her, "and you will be safe from the battles."

"I do not wish to be safe from the battles. These men are brave enough to risk their lives for the Confederacy," she told him. "It is my cause, too. The least I can do is aid them when they're wounded. I have a purpose here: I would have none, safe behind the lines."

She thought he flinched. "I have signed up to fight. I waited only for our wedding, then I shall leave New Orleans."

Victorine looked at him with a measure of respect. "I salute you for it. But you need not wait. I will not marry you, André. I wish you good fortune, but you already have one woman to weep for you when you leave. My husband, when I choose one, will love only me."

André stepped back into the saddle. "At the camp, you will find the bundle of clothes your father asked me to deliver, and letters with it. I have done everything a gentleman of honor can do. I trust you do not regret your rash actions!" He jerked on the reins; the horse tossed its head and trotted away.

Victorine took a deep breath. André's flushed

face, his arrogant tone, stayed with her. This was the man to whom she had planned to entrust her life and her happiness, simply because he danced well, had a handsome face, and spoke so charmingly?

"*Mais non*, I regret nothing," she said aloud, watching André ride out of her life.

Back in camp, she found the clothing and the letters. From her father she read a message of both affection and reproach.

Ma petite,
    I have been so worried. How can you choose to disregard my wishes? Come home at once with André; you must be married without delay. You risk your good reputation as well as your safety by traveling with the army!

Victorine sighed. Her father's distress grieved her, but her mind was made up. There were also letters from her friends. Colette was well; she and her family had returned to their New Orleans home.

    At least our home in the city still stands, but our Confederate money is worth nothing, and we have had to resort to the free market; it pains us to depend on charity. And oh, Victorine, we were forced to sign the pledge of alliance to the Union—I felt it like a blow to the heart. But otherwise, we wouldn't be allowed to stay in our own home. Beast Butler is still fighting his war against women—one woman was sent to prison for wearing a rebel flag on her dress!

And the Beast's brother is using the new Confiscation Act to seize and sell property of Southern sympathizers. Rumors say that his brother, the general, shares in the spoils, and both Butlers will become rich off the war.

My brother is safe. Maman and the children send their love. God keep you well. I think you are very brave.

Colette

Beast was an apt name, Victorine thought. Then, to her delight, she found a letter from Rosamund, sent on by her father.

Dearest Victorine,

One small consolation for being under Union control is that I can get a letter mailed to you. My family is holding on, though we have lost two more cows to our Yankee "protectors."

Those here who lost menfolk at Forts Donelson and Henry are not unhappy to hear that the once victorious Yankee general Grant is now in disgrace for being caught off guard at Shiloh, some even whispering that he was drunk.

It's rumored there has been a second Southern victory at Manassas, so a large part of Virginia is again safe from Union armies. Oh, I had a letter from Elizabeth —smuggled in and half of it so mangled it was impossible to read. I'm enclosing it for you.

Are you a married lady? Write to me if you can. I send you good wishes and the love of an old friend,

Rosamund

Elizabeth's letter was so smudged it was impossible to read in the dim light; Victorine put it aside to decipher later.

In the rest of the bundle she found three dresses to replace the stained and travel-worn frocks she had been wearing for weeks. Victorine was not so altered that she did not feel a ripple of pleasure as she shook out a handsome muslin skirt, pink and trimmed with white lace. For once Brent Whitman could see her in a more attractive guise. She did her hair with extra care and wore the dress when she joined him for their evening meal.

"You look very fine tonight." Though he bowed to her, his tone was grave.

Had she made a tactical error? Next to the faded uniforms around her, Victorine felt too fine, too luxurious. The dress was a hint of her old life in New Orleans, and it seemed to remind Dr. Whitman of the gulf between them.

When they had eaten, he asked her to walk a little way from the camp with him. Victorine agreed eagerly, hoping he would speak of his feelings, as he had been about to do the evening before. But his first words jolted her.

"I spoke briefly to Monsieur Valmont," the doctor said as they walked side by side through the deepening twilight. The air was soft and warm, and Victorine waved away a whining mosquito that buzzed near her cheek. "He said he is your fiancé."

Victorine shook her head vigorously. "*Mais non!* He was once, but I have told you, that is ended."

Some of the strain in the doctor's eyes eased, but he still did not smile. Victorine felt a wave of panic. What was wrong?

"But your father—he warned me away from you once. It is true, what they say about Creoles? Monsieur LaGrande would not allow an American to ask for your hand?"

Victorine's first thought was joyful. Brent did love her! The intensity of her response was almost a surprise—even in the first giddy days of André's courtship she had never felt this happy. It was as if her growth through hardship and danger had deepened her capacity to love—she was more truly a woman now, not a thoughtless girl. Her emotions were more powerful, her heart bigger. She could love this strong, gentle American as he deserved to be loved. "I would be most pleased!" she told him.

"But your father?" Brent Whitman's gaze was steady.

She could not lie to him. "No, he would not be happy. But it is my choice. I love you, Brent." There, she had said it. Victorine braced her shoulders and met his gaze firmly.

Dr. Whitman blinked, bent toward her, then shook his head. Instead of bestowing the kiss she had hoped for, he took her hand and held it tight. "My dearest Victorine, you are still very young."

"I am seventeen, eighteen in a month! That is not young. Many women are already married at my age."

"But you're not of legal age to marry without your father's permission. And you're far away from home, alone among strangers. How can I take such advantage? I cannot propose when I know your family would disapprove. I'm not Creole, and I'm not wealthy. I understand how they could think me a poor choice of suitor."

Victorine's vision blurred, and she blinked hard. How could she dissuade him? "Are you sending me away?"

"Would you go?" His voice was quiet.

"No!" She lifted her chin defiantly, despite the tears that threatened to overflow.

"Then I have no way to force you." He smiled, though his eyes were still sad.

Victorine's panic subsided. At least he was here, they were still together, and he held her hand firmly. But the words of love she knew were in his heart were still unspoken. She had sent away one fiancé, and now her new love, her real love, would not allow himself to speak.

Would she ever be allowed any happiness?

*C*hapter 16

"We're moving out," Brent Whitman told Victorine two days later. "General Breckinridge has been ordered north; some troops will remain here, but he wants me to go along. As for you—"

"Obviously he doesn't want to lose a good doctor," Victorine agreed. "And don't try to talk me out of going; you're wasting your time, *n'est-ce pas?*"

He gave her a reluctant smile. "Are you always this stubborn?"

"Only since I went to war." Victorine smiled back. "You look tired. I wish you'd had more time to rest."

She wanted to push back the strand of blond hair that fell across his forehead, but that would be too forward. When would she have the right to act as more than a friend?

Sighing, Victorine helped him pack, placing glass vials carefully in a fitted wood box. Meanwhile, Brent packed instruments into his leather travel case. The sharp clang of metal made Victorine look up, startled.

The doctor had dropped a sharp surgical knife; she watched him bend wearily to pick it up. "You're sure you're all right?" She thought his skin looked pasty.

"Just clumsy."

"You've been working too hard," she told him. "Perhaps you should ask the general to let you remain here."

He shook his head. "I'll go where I'm needed."

There was no arguing with him. At least she would be at his side. But hardly a day into the journey, at a brief rest stop, Dr. Whitman went to check on a private's injured ankle and collapsed in a heap.

Running to him, Victorine felt a stab of fear. When she touched his skin, it felt as if it might burn her hand. "Fever!" she exclaimed.

The news passed down the line, and General Breckinridge himself came back to see what the delay was.

"He cannot go on," Victorine insisted. "You must stop."

The Kentuckian with the straight nose and

high brow who had once served as vice-president of the United States sighed.

"Mademoiselle," he told Victorine, sounding much like her father, "I cannot halt an army for one man, as much as I value the captain. I have other doctors. If the captain cannot go on, he must be left behind."

"Then I will stay with him. He cannot be left alone," Victorine declared, "and he needs shelter. He cannot lie in the damp night air, with a fever already raging!"

The general sent out men who found them a tiny, apparently deserted cabin. Soon, with a little food and some medical supplies, Victorine was left alone with her patient. The man whose quiet strength had supported her through so many perils now lay on a crude cot, his body racked with fever.

She built a fire in the rough fireplace, boiled a kettle of water, and brewed tea. She gave him quinine and sips of herb tea, then used the rest of the cooled water to sponge his face and arms and chest.

The hours went by slowly. Once, when Brent lay quietly, Victorine took out her bag and reread all her recent letters, even straining her eyes over Elizabeth's mangled note. What did it say? She finally deciphered a few words.

> I think I have news of Adam, but it's
> Hannah who worries me now. . . .
> Hannah is in danger, and if I can't

The rest she couldn't make out. Hannah, the slave girl with the intelligent eyes and pleasing face—what could have happened to Hannah? But a groan from the cot made Victorine hurry to Brent's side, and she had no more time to puzzle over the letter.

She had nursed other patients, but this was different. She touched Brent Whitman's body tenderly, gently. His skin was tanned and his blond hair streaked by the sun. His arms and shoulders were corded with muscles built by lifting sick men. He had given so much for others, given so much to her, by his confidence in her ability and his thoughtful care for her needs.

As the night wore slowly on, Victorine memorized every line of his face, every angle of his body. She knew the tiny scar beneath his left eyebrow and the way his nostrils flared when he groaned, out of his head with fever. She fought the illness with the only means she had, and she prayed to God not to take away this man who meant so much to her, just when she had found him.

She sat on the dirt floor next to his rough cot.

When Brent was quiet, she leaned her head against his shoulder and dozed, knowing that when he moved she would wake and again offer him weak tea to drink, then sponge off his forehead, hot and dry as the fever came and went.

On the second night she thought he was lost to her. His fever seemed to rise; his body trembled with spasms. He spoke garbled sentences and stared at visions she couldn't see.

Victorine mixed the quinine, watching the level in her bottle dropping, hoping the medicine would last, hoping he could hold on. She sponged his face and chest again and again, sometimes holding him on the cot when he tried to twist away in his delirium.

Once he called out, "Victorine, dearest," and her heart ached. These were the words she had imagined hearing him speak, but not like this, in the grip of deadly illness.

When he fell back onto the blankets, she strained to see if his chest still rose and fell, touching his bare skin anxiously. If his heart had stopped, she thought her own would, too.

"Dear God, spare him," she whispered aloud, as she had prayed silently since his illness had struck.

He lay so still that she couldn't bear it. Then at last she felt the slow rise and fall of his chest, saw that he slept a more natural sleep than the fever had permitted. His fever had broken. She covered him quickly with a rough blanket, then sat back on the hard-packed earthen floor, leaned her head against his shoulder once more, and wept softly. This time her prayer was of thanksgiving; then she slept.

Victorine woke to the sound of blows on the rickety door. She looked first to her patient, who blinked, opened his eyes, and met her gaze. Brent Whitman looked puzzled. "What?" he murmured.

"It's all right," she told him. "You've been ill, but you're better now. Lie still."

The pounding came again. Scrambling to her feet, Victorine went to the front door, hoping desperately not to see a Union uniform when she opened it. But the sight that met her eyes was even more unexpected. "Papa!"

"You are safe?" He glared at her, his frown deep, his black coat covered with dust.

"Yes, of course, but—" She stared at her father, still almost mute with astonishment.

"Where is he?" Monsieur LaGrande stamped into the cabin, glancing from side to side as if expecting the devil himself to be hiding there.

"Papa, what are you doing here? You've not joined up?"

"Of course not," he told her. "We have great new victories in Virginia; that Robert E. Lee, he is winning the war for us. But me, I cannot celebrate because my daughter is disgraced."

Victorine felt her head spin. Southern victories? But she couldn't think about the war now. "How did you find us?"

"When you did not return with André, I had to come, *n'est-ce pas?* And when I located the troop, they said they had left you and this American alone in a cabin. I could not believe my ears. How long have you been here?"

Victorine tried to think. "Three days, I think, but—"

"This is not to be heard of! A respectable woman, unmarried, alone with a man? What will your aunts and your cousins say? My poor daughter, you have been misled. Where is this villain?"

"Papa! You don't understand. Brent has been ill."

"Brent, eh?" Her father stood over the cot and glared down at the sick man. Brent Whitman looked back at him, his brow furrowed as if he didn't understand.

Victorine felt almost as confused. Yet for an instant she saw the little cabin through her father's eyes, saw the single tumbled bed, saw

Brent bare to the waist, covered only by the blanket. She couldn't keep herself from blushing.

"You have compromised my daughter's good name," Monsieur LaGrande told the sick man frostily. "You have no choice; if you are a gentleman, you must offer her your hand in marriage."

"Papa!" Embarrassed beyond words, Victorine grabbed her father's arm and by sheer determination propelled him back to the doorway. "Where is your horse? Ah, I see. Do you have any provisions? We are almost out of food."

"I have supplies in my saddlebags," Monsieur LaGrande told her.

"Then bring them; I will make some tea and fix us a meal. Then we'll talk about this calmly."

Her father glared; she stood her ground.

"Eh bien," he agreed, his shoulders sagging. "I am an old man, and tired, and the world is not the way it should be. But I will not see my only daughter disgraced; you must be married. I suppose this man is a heathen?"

"Of course not," she told him, with dignity. "You saw him at mass, remember? Brent is a proper Catholic."

She coaxed the dying embers of the fire back to life, feeding it carefully with small twigs until the flame caught and she could add bigger logs.

She cooked a simple meal, making gruel and more tea for Brent. Then she sent her father out to gather more firewood.

"But I am not a laborer," Monsieur LaGrande protested, looking insulted.

"You're the only one we have." Victorine smiled at him. "Papa, I have learned to do many things. Do you wish me to gather wood?"

"Of course not. This is what comes of leaving your home." Still grumbling, he went out of the cabin.

Feeling a pang of guilt, Victorine followed him outside. "Papa"—she put one hand on his arm—"I'm very sorry I have worried you. But there comes a time when I must follow my own conscience; can you understand that?"

He shook his head. "A woman does not think for herself—how could that be?"

Victorine sighed. "Then it grieves me that we cannot agree. But I love you, Papa, always."

He seemed to relent; he bent to kiss her forehead. "I, too, *ma petite*. You are always my daughter, and much loved, even when you act like a bold American!"

Smiling a little, she left him to gather wood and went back inside. At last she was able to sit beside Brent and speak privately. "You must not mind my father," she told him in a low tone. "He lives by an old code."

"He is a gentleman; I understand that," Brent told her, some of the old sparkle back in his eyes. Much of his face was covered by a ragged blond stubble, but the improvement in his health and spirits made him look beautiful to her. "He is concerned for you, naturally."

Victorine nodded. "But this threat, you must not heed it. I mean—" Stumbling over her words, she was vexed to find that she was blushing again. "I want no husband who is forced to the altar," she said more firmly.

Brent smiled up at her. Although still weak, he was able to reach for her hand. "You are the joy of my life and have been since I saw you that night at Mardi Gras. I have dreaded losing you more than any general fears defeat in battle. I can think of no greater privilege than to become your husband."

"*Vraiment?* Truly?" Victorine felt a rush of happiness. She lifted his hand and held it to her cheek.

"If you'll have me. I'm still only a poor doctor, without wealth or family connections, dearest, and we don't know where this war will lead. But you are the only woman I have loved, and the only one I wish to share my life with."

He brushed her cheek with his hand, his touch gentle yet intimate. It made her heart sing.

Savoring his caress, she closed her eyes for an instant, then opened them quickly to be sure she wasn't dreaming. "I love you, Brent. I will be most happy to become your wife," she whispered.

They were holding hands when her father returned with an armload of branches, but Victorine did not jump up. She smiled at her father, too happy for any pretense.

"Papa, we are to be married!"

"Of course, didn't I say so?" Monsieur LaGrande responded, his tone still haughty.

Victorine laughed softly, and Brent's grip on her hand tightened.

Where the war would lead, what the Confederacy's fate would be, she couldn't know. But Victorine had no fears as long as she and Brent could face the future together. This time she had made no mistake; this man she would love forever.

The SOUTHERN ANGELS saga continues with Hannah's story.

❊ *A Dream of Freedom*

Hannah, a slave from the Stafford plantation in Virginia, vows never to marry or even fall in love until she is free. Then Hannah is sent to work in Charleston, where she helps slaves find freedom through the Underground Railroad, and where she meets Joshua, a free man of color, whose love and devotion overwhelm her. Just as Joshua offers to save the money to buy Hannah's freedom, William Stafford summons Hannah back to the plantation. But Hannah continues to work on the Underground Railroad in Virginia—until the night Joshua comes for her and they make a daring attempt to flee north with a group of slaves. When Stafford stops them, Hannah finds herself on the auction block, further than ever from freedom and marriage to Joshua. Will her dream that all slaves be free cost Hannah her own liberty—and the love of her life?

❦ *About the Author* ❦

Born in Tennessee, CHERYL ZACH grew up in various areas of the South and has also lived in southern California and in Europe. She is a former teacher with an M.A. in English and has a son, daughter, and two stepsons. The author of thirty books for children and young adults, Ms. Zach spent three years traveling, researching, and writing the Southern Angels series. Here's what she has to say:

"I've always found historical sagas to be rich in drama, romance, and excitement. Civil War teens, much like modern young adults, needed courage, initiative, and compassion to overcome the dangers around them. I feel a great bond with those Southern angels of yesterday, who survived, endured, and despite danger and adversity often triumphed, giving us hope that we can do the same today. I hope they touch your hearts as well."